PROMISES
I Made

Also by
Michelle Zink

Lies I Told
A Temptation of Angels
This Wicked Game

PROPHECY OF THE SISTERS TRILOGY
Prophecy of the Sisters
Guardian of the Gate
Circle of Fire

PROMISES
I Made

MICHELLE ZINK

An Imprint of HarperCollins*Publishers*

HarperTeen is an imprint of HarperCollins Publishers.

Library of Congress Cataloging-in-Publication Data
Zink, Michelle.
   Promises I made / Michelle Zink. — First edition.
      pages   cm
   Sequel to: Lies I told.
   Summary: When Grace Fontaine leaves her "father" in Seattle, where he is working another con, and returns to Playa Hermosa, she receives help from unexpected sources in her quest to find information about Cormac and Renee that she can trade for her adopted brother Parker's freedom.
   ISBN 978-0-06-232715-4 (hardcover)
   [1. Conduct of life—Fiction.   2. Swindlers and swindling—Fiction.   3. Interpersonal relations—Fiction.   4. Criminal investigation—Fiction.   5. Brothers and sisters—Fiction. 6. Adoption—Fiction.]
PZ7.Z652Pp   2015   2014041204
[Fic]—dc23   CIP
                                                   AC

Typography by Torborg Davern
15 16 17 18 19   CG/RRDH   10 9 8 7 6 5 4 3 2 1

First Edition

For Charles and Margurite Baker, who taught us all
what it means to keep a promise

Everyone's a millionaire where promises are concerned.
—*Ovid*

Prologue

When I think about what happened in Playa Hermosa, it's not the gold that gets me. Gold is like money. Something tangible that can be obtained, lost, regained.

But trust, faith, love . . . Well, those things are a lot more tricky. Where do you find trust once it's lost? How do you make someone believe in you when you've given them every reason not to? And how can someone love you when you've proved beyond a shadow of a doubt that doing so is dangerous to them, and to everything and everyone they love?

Those are the kinds of things I thought about after Cormac and I arrived in Seattle. I was too numb to do much thinking before then, too focused on the growing distance between Parker and me, too busy imagining him in jail for a crime we'd all committed.

And then there was my mother. Renee. All the times she'd

called me Gracie. All the times she'd pushed the hair out of my eyes, called me her daughter. It had been a lie. Of course, I'd known Cormac and Renee weren't my biological parents. That Parker and I had been adopted by them to run cons with wealthy suburbanites as our victims. But somehow I'd believed that Renee loved me. That she was my mother in every important sense of the word. I'd believed it even when Parker had called me out on my naivety, even when it set me against him, the one person who'd proved over and over that he'd do anything for me.

Knowing that Renee had taken the gold left me hollowed out, like all the little bits of love and security and hope I'd been accumulating had been sucked out of me all at once. I thought it would get better with time, that I'd adjust to the reality of the situation like I'd always done before. But this time was different. The emptiness was palpable, a black hole that seemed to gather more power with each passing day. Sometimes I thought I would disappear inside it completely.

We'd all sacrificed in the name of the Playa Hermosa con. Cormac was on the run, forced to be cautious even with the underground network of contacts we usually relied on. With twenty million dollars in gold at stake; there had to be at least a few fellow grifters who would use information about our whereabouts as a get-out-of-jail-free card. In the meantime, that's where Parker was: in jail. I hadn't seen or talked to him since the night of the Fairchild con. I didn't even dare send him a letter, and the loss of him sat like a lead weight on my chest.

My sacrifices might seem insignificant in comparison, but they didn't feel that way. I'd come to love Selena, the only real friend I'd ever had. And I loved Logan Fairchild and his parents, too. Stealing from them—especially with the knowledge of Warren Fairchild's mental illness—had blown out the tiny light I'd kept burning in the darkest corners of my heart. The light that told me I was better than a life on the grift, that I was only doing it because I had to, because after a string of lousy foster homes and no contact with my real parents, Cormac, Renee, and Parker were the only family I had.

Parker had tried to show me the better parts of myself, to keep those parts alive, and I'd abandoned him in Los Angeles when I'd chosen to run with Cormac. Now I knew the truth about who I was, and I didn't waste any more time trying to fight it. I spent the time in Seattle settling into the role of Cormac's daughter as he worked to con a rich divorcée, hoping to get us flush enough to go after Renee and our share of the Playa Hermosa take. In the meantime, I waited for Cormac to follow through on his promise to get help for Parker, to go back for him or find him a lawyer, to do *something* to get him out of jail. I waited for nearly five months, until I couldn't wait any longer. Until the thought of Parker locked up started to unravel me.

Then I used everything Cormac and Renee had taught me and I did it myself.

One

I waited until Cormac and Miranda left for the theater to steal the money. I didn't know how much we had left; I wasn't even entirely sure where Cormac kept it. But I knew he'd had to liquidate the single gold bar left by Renee to fund the Seattle job, and I knew he was super paranoid. That made me think he was keeping the money close, that he wouldn't risk a bank, even with the new IDs he'd managed to get us through one of the few sources he still trusted. It was one of the reasons he'd chosen Seattle; the last job we'd done there had only lasted two months—long enough to make a few connections but not so long that we were well known in the area.

I stayed in my room until I heard the front door shut, then went to the window, watching as Cormac opened the passenger door of Miranda's Mercedes. Miranda climbed in, long red hair brushing across her ivory shoulders, bare except for the thin straps of her green gown. She laughed up at Cormac, handsome as ever in a custom tux Miranda had bought him after he surprised her with season tickets to the ballet.

Guilt plucked at my insides. Like all the people we'd stolen from, Miranda was just trying to find some kind of happiness. Sure, she was rich, if only because her ex-husband, William Mayer, was a real estate developer responsible for half the skyscrapers in downtown Seattle.

But I'd learned the hard way that money didn't tell the whole story, and I felt bad about what Cormac was doing to her. What we were both doing to her. She'd already suffered a high-profile divorce after William was caught having an affair with their daughter's twenty-year-old best friend. Miranda had gotten a hefty settlement, but what good did that do her? Did it make her less ashamed when she saw her family on the front page? Did it lessen her daughter's embarrassment at college?

I doubted it.

And now Cormac and I had moved into Miranda's mansion overlooking Lake Washington, and if Cormac had his way, we'd add insult to injury by stealing what little she had left: her financial security.

I was doing Miranda a favor by stealing Cormac's money. Our money. Maybe he wouldn't be able to keep up the ruse. Maybe she'd figure out that he wasn't a rich tech refugee who'd left the business after selling his start-up for millions of dollars. Maybe she'd even figure it out in time to stop him. But I doubted it. Cormac always landed on his feet. The rest of us were just there to break his fall.

Cormac closed the passenger door and hurried around to the driver's side of the Mercedes. Even now he had the walk of someone who had it all, someone who'd always had it all. Fit and trim in his tux, dark hair just beginning to gray near his temples, he didn't look any worse for wear after Renee's betrayal.

I knew I couldn't say the same. I'd lost weight since coming to Seattle. A lot of weight. My old clothes had hung on me until Miranda insisted on taking me shopping, and my pale face stood out in stark contrast to my newly dyed black hair, a color that only served to bring out the smudges taking up residence under my eyes. It didn't matter. I avoided mirrors now. I didn't recognize the reflection. I wasn't sure I wanted to.

I watched Cormac back out of the driveway, then reached for the backpack I'd stuffed into my closet. It had the few things I needed and the even fewer things that mattered to me: some clothes and toiletries, my laptop, a leather bracelet I'd found in a surf shop in Bellevue that reminded me of the ones Parker wore to cover up his scars, my wallet with my Seattle driver's license in the name of Julie Montrose.

Before Playa Hermosa, we'd always kept the same first names for continuity, and Parker and I had been immediately enrolled in the local high school of whatever town we were working. But in Seattle, Cormac was running scared, unsure how much the police would be able to get out of Parker. We had to use different first names, and to avoid the exposure of enrolling me in school he'd told Miranda that I'd graduated from high school the year before and was taking a gap year before college. I'd spent the last three months of what should have been my junior year reading in my room while endless rain beaded the windows, leaving the house only to take long walks in Bellevue Square, sitting on the benches that lined the shores of the lake while rain pattered against my Windbreaker. The house and town had become a kind of purgatory, a place where there was no past and no future. Just minutes stretching into hours stretching into days. Part of me wanted to stay here forever. I was so tired. So, so tired. The thought of making my way back to Los Angeles, of trying to figure out a way to help Parker, made me want to curl into a ball and sleep forever.

But then I'd think of Parker in jail. I'd remember his words to me during our last phone call the night of the Fairchild con: *It's you and me. No matter what.* Then the urge to reach him would become almost unbearable, and I'd have to force myself to stay put. To wait until I had a plan.

Finally I'd admitted that I would never have a plan. Not an airtight one. I had no idea how much money Cormac had left. No idea if Selena would help me or how I would even communicate with Parker without being taken into custody myself. But I couldn't count on Cormac, and I couldn't stay in the guest bedroom at Miranda's house forever. Making a move was the only choice I had left.

I watched the Mercedes disappear around the corner, then headed for the hallway.

The house was quiet as I made my way down the stairs to the big master bedroom. I'd never lived in a house where the master was on the first floor, but here it was, right off the formal living room that no one used. I hurried past the front door, crossed the foyer, and opened one of the double doors.

I'd only ever glimpsed the room from the doorway on the couple of occasions I'd had to ask Cormac something. Then I had waited for him to come to the door, cringing, trying not to think about what he and Miranda were doing in there. Con or no con, his relationship with her still felt like a betrayal of Renee, which was crazy under the circumstances. Proof that I was fucked in the head.

I stood in the doorway and looked around the room, trying to get my bearings. There was a giant Cal king bed covered in an understated floral duvet, two nightstands, a massive armoire that I knew housed the television and media equipment, and two large dressers. Some kind of filmy nightgown lay across an upholstered bench at the foot of the bed, and a pair of oxfords that I recognized as Cormac's stood neatly in front of one of the walk-in closets.

I started with the nightstands. I didn't expect the money to be there; Cormac was better than that. But I'd learned to rule out the obvious first, then to move toward the more obscure possibilities.

The nightstand on the left must have been Cormac's. It

contained two financial-type books with men in suits on the cover, a pack of breath mints, a stress ball, nail clippers, and, much to my horror, a half-used package of condoms. I pulled out the drawer and checked the underside, then felt in the back of the compartment for something that might be taped there.

Nothing.

I replaced the drawer and moved to the other night table. Hand cream, two nail files, a hairbrush, a journal, some old birthday cards, lip balm, and, surprisingly, an inhaler. I hadn't been aware that Miranda had asthma.

I closed the drawer and made my way methodically around the room. Mattress (between it and the box spring), dressers (check drawers for a false bottom, remove them to see if something is taped inside, pull them away from the wall to see if something is hidden behind them), closets (look behind clothes and inside shoes, and scan the walls for a safe or a hidden panel), armoire (check behind everything, including the TV, and in the drawers that house DVDs). Finally I looked under the bench at the foot of the bed, catching a whiff of Miranda's perfume, grassy and fresh, when I moved the nightgown.

Nothing.

I stood there, looking around the room, trying to figure out what I'd missed. Cormac would want to keep the money close in case we had to run. It had to be here.

My gaze landed on everything I'd already checked: closets, dressers, bench, bed, nightstands.

Nightstands.

I'd removed the drawer in the nightstand that was

obviously Cormac's, but I hadn't done the same for the one on Miranda's side of the bed. Subconsciously I'd assumed he wouldn't go to the trouble of putting it somewhere that might be difficult to access, but maybe in such tight quarters the allure of an unlikely hiding spot outweighed the fact that it was a few feet away from where he slept.

I moved across the room and pulled out the nightstand drawer. After setting it on the floor, I reached into the back of the drawer compartment and felt around. It only took me a second to find the smooth rectangle stuck to the back. Now that I'd discovered it, I wasn't surprised. It was just like Cormac to play that kind of head game, to hide something right under the nose of the person who might be looking for it. He probably felt a little thrill of excitement every time Miranda opened her nightstand, more proof that he was smarter and better than the rest of us.

I felt for the edge of the paper and pulled. It came away with a soft rip, and when I had it in my hand, I saw that it was an envelope, tacky along the outside edges where the tape had held it in place.

My heart beat wildly as I slipped a finger under the seal. When it was open, I removed a stack of bills that wasn't nearly as thick as it should have been, then started counting, piling hundreds on the plush white carpet.

I was halfway through the stack when dread began to bloom in my chest. By the time I was done counting, my breath was coming fast and shallow.

Twenty-nine hundred dollars.

That was all that was left of the gold Cormac had

liquidated a little less than five months ago. He'd been secretive about the sale price, but when I looked online, the price of a gold bar had been somewhere around thirty-five thousand dollars. Even allowing for the fact that he'd probably had to sell it through a commodities fence, he must have cleared thirty thousand and change. Which meant we'd gone through a lot of money since leaving Playa Hermosa.

True, we'd spent a month in a hotel and another in a high-end condo on the water before we'd moved in with Miranda. We'd needed clothes and food, and Cormac had leased a car through a shady series of arrangements that took us from an auto mechanic in Bothell to a BMW dealership downtown. All in the name of the con, of course. All in the name of getting Miranda to see Cormac as the wealthy entrepreneur he claimed to be.

I should have expected us to be almost out of money. Still, it came as a shock, and I hesitated over the stacks of bills, wondering if I should leave Cormac something, before putting them all back in the envelope and stuffing it quickly into my backpack.

Cormac had used more than his share of the money to rebound. Parker had gone to jail for it and hadn't seen a dime. I'd use every cent of what was left to get him out of trouble if I could, and I wouldn't waste any more time feeling bad for Cormac.

He was on his own now.

We all were.

Two

I took a cab into downtown Bellevue, then hopped a bus to the Amtrak station on King Street. Taking a bus to Los Angeles would have been faster by a few hours, but the truth is, I needed the extra time. I had only the vaguest of ideas about what to do after I got back to LA. I needed every hour to come up with a plan.

The train didn't leave until 9:35 the next morning, so I got a room in a crappy motel near the station, then walked to a market to stock up on snacks and bottled water for the trip. I'd read online that the train had a dining car and a lounge, both of which offered food, but I wanted to minimize my exposure. I wasn't worried about Cormac coming after me; he wouldn't risk hunting me down for such a measly amount of money. But the Fairchild con had been big news in Southern California. Our pictures—old and new—had been plastered all over the newspapers. I had spent hours poring over the articles in the motel room we'd lived in while Cormac was scamming for a new mark. And while I didn't think I looked like Grace Fontaine anymore—like the person who'd been best friends with Selena Rodriguez, who'd fallen in love with Logan Fairchild—I wasn't sure enough to bet my freedom on it. Not until I'd helped Parker.

I stuffed my purchases into my backpack and then stopped at a diner, where I bought two grilled-cheese sandwiches and fries to go. It was weird to be out in public after months of being cooped up in Miranda's house or walking the waterfront alone. Now everything seemed a little too bright, a little too loud. I had to push away the feeling that everyone was looking at me, that they all knew what I'd done to Logan and his family. That the police would show up any minute and take me away before I had time to go back for Parker. I was relieved to get back to my room, even with the dim lighting and the slight smell of mildew and dust.

I used a proxy server to search online for recent news about Parker while I ate my dinner. A VPN would have been better—some of them didn't keep logs—but I needed a credit card to access them. I made a mental note to pick up a prepaid card somewhere along the way.

Nothing new had developed in Parker's case since the last time I'd combed the internet for information about him. He was being held in Los Angeles County Jail. The judge had cited flight risk as a reason to refuse bail, and Parker had been assigned a public defender named Robin Mannheim and charged with three counts of felony fraud and one count of grand theft. I knew that the guard from Allied Security had died following a gunshot to his chest. The prosecutor had tried to pin it on Parker but couldn't for lack of evidence, which made perfect sense given the blood on Cormac's shirt the night we stole Warren's gold. Cormac hadn't admitted it, but I knew he'd been the one to shoot the guard. Parker was already on the run by then. Still, the state expected more charges against him pending their investigation. None of it was a surprise, but I had to fight against despair as I closed my computer. How was I supposed to help Parker? I couldn't even visit him in jail without being taken into custody, and then we'd both be screwed. Because one thing I now knew for sure: Cormac and Renee weren't going to lift a finger to help either of us.

I spent a fitful night drifting in the ether between wakefulness and sleep. A sliver of light from the walkway outside sneaked in between the polyester curtains, and I could hear people talking as they passed by my room. At one point, two people stopped outside the door, throwing shadows under it, and I sat up in bed in a panic, listening as they engaged in murmured conversation. When they didn't move on, I jumped out of bed, stuffing my feet into my shoes and grabbing my backpack and laptop, wondering how long it would be before whoever it was broke down the door and came in after me. I felt stupid when their voices faded away a few minutes later, but I wasn't able to go back to sleep afterward. I turned on the TV instead and watched reruns of *Full House* while the hours ticked by.

I left the room just after nine a.m. and headed to the train station. I held my breath as I slid my driver's license under the ticket window, glad the birth date on Julie Montrose's ID made me eighteen on the Washington State driver's license. A moment later, the gray-haired ticket attendant passed back my change along with my ticket to LA.

I avoided eye contact with the other passengers as I followed the signs to my platform, but I kept my head up. If you act guilty of something, people will remember you, think you *are* guilty of something. Another lesson from Cormac and Renee. I tried to maintain an expression of boredom as I climbed onto the train and looked for a seat, surprised to find that they all swiveled to face the windows. It wasn't nearly as private as I'd expected, and I chose a seat at the end of an empty row, hoping it would stay that way. Then I put in my headphones as a deterrent against conversation.

I kept my eyes on the concrete platform, half expecting someone official-looking to come running for the train at the last minute, holding a flyer with my face plastered all over it. The thought made my heart beat too fast and my skin prickle with nervousness. I'd never been afraid when traveling with Cormac and Renee, even as we changed names and hair colors, addresses and IDs. Somehow they always made me feel like we had every right to be wherever we were. Now I didn't know if it had been a gift or a curse. The safety had been nice, but they had been wrong. We were thieves and liars. We didn't have any rights at all.

I watched a bearded guy on the platform clasp an older man's hand, then draw him into an embrace. A moment later he bent to a slight woman with shining eyes and enveloped her in his arms. When they parted, he grabbed an over-stuffed backpack and gave the couple a final wave before disappearing into one of the cars at the front of the train. I watched the couple walk away, arms around each other's waists.

A crackly voice came over the loudspeaker welcoming us aboard the train from Seattle to Los Angeles. I scanned the aisle while I listened to the emergency instructions and was relieved when no one took the seat next to me. I wasn't up to polite conversation, and I didn't want to spend the next thirty-five hours wondering if the person next to me would have a sudden epiphany and recognize my face.

The loudspeaker grew silent, and a few minutes later the train shifted and began to move.

The rocking motion was unsettling at first. The train was moving forward, but it also swayed slightly under my body. I had the odd sensation of being on a boat and in a car at the same time. Then we broke free of the station, and everything smoothed out as we picked up speed.

We moved through the city and past Tacoma, the waters of the Puget Sound glimmering dark under the rising sun. It made me think of Playa Hermosa, of the Cove and the feel of Logan's hand in mine, the way Selena smiled when she made some wry observation, like it was a secret just between us. I was homesick for all of it, which didn't make any sense.

We'd only lived there for three months. How was it possible that it felt like home?

I grew drowsy, the rhythmic sway of the train lulling me into a pleasant fog, and I finally fell asleep with my backpack in my lap, the morning sun warming my body through the big east-facing windows. Every time the train stopped to let passengers on or off, I jerked awake, fear winding sharp and fast through my body. Had Cormac sent someone to find me after all? Had the police somehow subverted my use of a proxy on the internet? I had no idea what kind of resources were used to catch a criminal like me, and I couldn't shake the feeling that I was on borrowed time, that my freedom would be short-lived outside of Cormac's protection.

By the time we reached Portland, Oregon, I'd settled into a routine: waking up when we stopped, keeping my stuff close in case I had to run, eating something from my stash, dozing off when we were safely in motion. I took everything with me when I had to use the restroom and made a point of finding a new place to sit when I was done. People came and went in the seats next to me. Old people, young people. Men, women, and once a small girl traveling with her mother, clutching a coloring book and a plastic bag full of crayons. I gave each of them a polite smile and turned back to the book in my hands, rereading the same ten pages across eleven hundred miles. Time was my enemy. There were endless amounts of it, hour upon hour when there was nothing to do but think of Logan. I still felt a hitch in my breath at the thought of him, still felt the hollow place throb in my chest when I remembered his arms around me. I noticed his absence constantly, like those people you hear about who lose a limb but still feel it ache when it rains. I tried to focus instead on coming up with a plan to rescue Parker, but my mind drew a blank. I never got past the point where I arrived in LA with no place to sleep and no one to call for help.

We pulled into Union Station just after one a.m., a little over twenty-four hours after we'd left Seattle. My body was stiff and a little sore as I grabbed my stuff and disembarked the train, and my footsteps echoed across the cavernous rooms as I made my way through the old building. The stained-glass windows were dark overhead, the ceiling rising so high that I almost couldn't see it beyond the shadows. The station was nearly deserted, but I stayed alert anyway, my gaze skimming over the few people who sat on benches or leaned against the wall. Now was not the time to be sloppy.

I stepped out into a cool California night. It was mid-May, and the heat of summer hadn't yet settled into the concrete. I felt a pang of fear when I realized there were no cabs outside the station, no buses, no people. Just a big empty parking lot sporadically lit with streetlamps and a neighborhood that looked like it had seen better days.

I walked to the sidewalk and headed for the corner, looking around for a hotel. I hadn't gone a block when I passed a group of men leaning in the shadows of a crumbling brick building. They called softly to me as I passed.

"Hey, pretty mama . . ."

"All alone?"

"*Oye, muchacha bonita.*"

I was suddenly aware of how alone I was, how vulnerable. No one in the world knew where I was. No one cared. I'd left my cell phone in Bellevue in case Cormac tried to track me with it. I could disappear off the face of the earth and no one would even notice.

I turned and headed back for the station, remembering a bank of pay phones near the exit. I couldn't afford to get mugged in some back alley. Who would help Parker then?

I located the phones and was reading the directions to dial information (who knew you could dial 411 for information? Would it be the kind of information that would find me a cab? A motel?) when I noticed a sticker advertising a taxi service. It was half peeled off, but I could still make out the number. I dug in my pocket for some change and dialed.

The dispatcher said it would be twenty minutes, so I waited inside the station, watching out the window until fifteen minutes had passed. Then I ventured outside, careful to stay under one of the streetlights near the parking lot. A couple of minutes later a yellow taxi came to a stop at the curb.

I slid into the backseat, tugging my backpack in after me. The driver was a middle-aged woman, her dark hair pulled into a ponytail. She held one hand near the cracked window, a swirl of smoke rising from a cigarette in her long fingers.

"Where we headed, honey?" she asked.

"Torrance." I said it almost without thinking, but then I realized it was the perfect place. Only fifteen minutes from Playa Hermosa, Torrance was clean and suburban, big enough to get lost in but not too big for comfort. I didn't know what I'd do once I got there, but it was close enough to Playa Hermosa that I could move quickly once I figured it out.

"You got it," the driver said, pulling out of the parking lot. "I'm Meg. You just get into town?"

"Yep." It was best to say as little as possible when you were on the run. It was too easy to babble when you were scared or nervous, too easy to let something slip. Even something small could be your ruin on the grift.

"Where you from?" She met my gaze in the rearview mirror, and I tried to see myself through her eyes: a tough girl with eyes that told too many sad stories.

"Chicago," I said.

"Got family out here?" I sensed a little desperation in her voice as she realized small talk wasn't exactly my forte.

I shook my head. "I'm meeting up with friends. We're going to Mexico." The lie came easily.

"Ah, Mexico." I heard the smile in her voice. "What I wouldn't give to be young and in Mexico again."

I smiled politely and put in my earbuds, then turned my face to the window. My survival depended on making as few connections as possible now that I was close to the scene of our crime. And so did Parker's.

We wound our way through the city and got onto one of LA's freeways. It was nearly two, and the roads were strangely deserted, the streetlamps casting yellow orbs onto the pavement. The lights on the skyscrapers downtown faded away in favor of concrete that seemed to stretch in every direction, crammed tightly with houses and asphalt, mini-malls, and fast-food restaurants, a few palm trees dotting the streets like candles on an otherwise bland birthday cake. It was hard to believe that Playa Hermosa was less than an hour away. That the tropical refuge filled with wild parrots and peacocks, the sea crashing against the cliff at the base of the peninsula, could exist hand in hand with the concrete jungle that was Los Angeles and its surrounding suburbs.

The taxi driver put on her blinker and looked at me in the rearview mirror as she prepared to exit the freeway. "So where exactly am I dropping you?"

I hesitated for a split second. "I think I'm the first one here. If you could get me to a cheap hotel in the area, I'll text my friends and let them know where I am."

She nodded. "You looking for something by the mall? Or closer to the beach?"

I had a flash of the Cove in Playa Hermosa, the water rushing up the sand, the rise and fall of it, the softest of sighs.

"The mall is fine." I didn't need the memories of the ocean, and I didn't want to risk running into Logan or any of the guys. They usually surfed at the Cove, but I'd heard them mention moving north to Torrance or Redondo Beach when the swells were better there.

We continued up Hawthorne Boulevard, past the Galleria mall, where Selena and I went shopping on the day we really became friends. Other than Parker, she was the only person I'd ever gotten close to, the only person I'd really let in. I wondered what she had done with my betrayal. If she replayed our time together, searching for clues, blaming herself for not seeing it sooner. I hoped not. It wasn't her fault. No one ever saw us coming. That was why Cormac and Renee needed Parker and me so much. We made them look normal, allowed them to hide behind the façade of a picture-perfect family.

"How's that?" the driver said, tipping her head at an Econo Lodge on the corner. "Close to everything, probably cheap."

"Great, thanks," I said.

The car dipped as she pulled into the hotel parking lot. I looked at the meter and dug in my bag for money, then passed it over the seat with an extra five dollars when she stopped in front of the lobby. Five dollars was on the low end of fair for a tip, but perfectly appropriate for someone my age. I didn't want to stand out as some kind of teenage high roller.

"Have a great time in Mexico," Meg said as I opened the door. "But keep your wits about you. It can be as dangerous as it is beautiful."

I watched her go, the words ringing in my ears.

Three

I walked about a half a mile before I saw a Motel 6. I could have stayed at the Econo Lodge, but I didn't want to risk some kind of belated recognition on the part of the taxi driver. The streets were empty except for the traffic whizzing past in both directions, but I wasn't afraid here. I could smell the ocean even from Hawthorne Boulevard, feel the briny weight of it, and I felt safe against all reason.

The hotel was comfortingly nondescript, the white tile floors polished to an antiseptic shine, the walls filled with generic prints of the ocean. It was after three in the morning, and the only person in the lobby was a guy in his twenties, clean-cut and wearing a name tag that read *Brad*, who was manning the front desk. I told him I was a light sleeper and requested a room at the end of the hall. Then I handed over my Seattle ID and paid for two nights.

I took an elevator to the second floor and followed the brass placards pointing toward my room number. Being at the end of the hall would serve more than one purpose: I would be able to get out fast if the situation called for it, and I could use the stairwell instead of the elevator without having to walk past a bunch of different rooms. All of which meant less exposure, fewer people who could identity me if things went bad.

I used my key card to enter the room and locked the door, finishing with the brass bar at the top. Turning on the lights, I scanned the room. Closet just outside the bathroom on my immediate left, dresser with TV and mini coffeemaker, bed, two nightstands, small table and chairs by the window.

I dropped my backpack on the bed and crossed the room. Pulling back the curtain, I wasn't surprised to see that the window didn't open. That was standard for hotel rooms, whose parent companies didn't want to be sued when people got drunk or careless. The same was true for balconies, which Cormac had told me most hotels used to have but which were now all but obsolete.

I looked past the parking lot at the sparse traffic moving below, the ocean a blank space beyond the city. Exhaustion, heavy and suffocating, fell over me like a wet blanket. I hadn't slept well on the train, and the last time I'd been in a bed had been at the crappy motel in Seattle two nights ago. There were things I needed to do, but I wouldn't be able to deal with any of them if I didn't get some sleep.

I pulled the curtains closed and headed for the bathroom,

where I took a long, hot shower. I threw on the only paja-mas I'd brought, a pair of loose boxer shorts and a tank top, and stared at my face in the mirror as I combed through my short, choppy hair. Usually, my blue eyes were the one thing that brought me back to myself. I might change my hair for the con, and I often changed the kind of clothes I wore to fit in with our mark. But my eyes were the one thing that always stayed the same. Now I hardly recognized myself in them. They were still blue, but there was a deadness there I hadn't seen before. Or maybe, like so many things, I'd just never looked hard enough to notice.

I turned away from the mirror. Then I shut off the light and fell into bed.

Four

The curtains in the hotel room blocked out everything so that I was only dimly aware of the passing of time. I woke up to go to the bathroom, and once to guzzle from one of the water bottles I still had in my backpack. The room was always dark, although at some point I woke to find a sliver of gold shining through a crack in the curtains, the only indication of daylight outside the room. My limbs felt heavy, like I was moving underwater, and while I knew I needed to wake up, to do something, I could never do more than fall back into the pillowy hotel bed. For a while, nothing seemed to exist outside of the bland room, and I twice turned away knocks for housekeeping. I didn't want to leave my sleep-fueled delirium. Everything was so much easier when all you had to worry about was going to the bathroom or getting a drink of water.

Finally I opened my eyes and knew that I was awake, really awake, for the first time in days. Hunger gnawed at my stomach, and my lips were chapped from the air conditioner.

I picked up the complimentary newspaper outside my door and looked at the date. May thirteenth. I'd been asleep for two whole days. Two days that Parker had been in jail. Two days when I'd done nothing to get him out.

The thought mobilized me. I took another shower and put on cargo capris and a tank top. They had once been part of my uniform in Playa Hermosa, but I'd had to ditch them for the black jeans and dark sweaters that became part of my Seattle persona. I felt exposed in my California clothes, the antithesis of the rocker hair and dark eyeliner I'd been wearing since Christmas, but I didn't want to stand out too much while I was here.

When I was dressed, I packed everything into my backpack and left the room. I couldn't risk leaving my stuff just in case someone discovered my whereabouts while I was out. I had to be mobile, ready to run and hide, at all times.

I stopped at the front desk and paid for one more night, trying not to stress as I peeled another hundred and twenty dollars from the stack of bills I'd stolen from Cormac. Then I walked to the Denny's next door and chose a seat in the back, as far from the windows as I could get.

I ordered a giant breakfast of blueberry pancakes, scrambled eggs, bacon, toast, and black coffee before taking my notebook out of my bag and starting the lists I would need to organize the next phase of my mission. The first one was easy. *Things I Need:* a track phone, a prepaid credit card, a new ID, sunglasses, laundry soap, a few toiletries.

The next one was a lot harder.

I wrote *WICDTHP* at the top of the second page. It stood for *What I Can Do to Help Parker,* but I didn't dare spell it out in case I was caught by the police.

I was still staring at the blank page when the waitress brought my food. I closed my notebook and leaned back in the booth while she set all the plates and a carafe of coffee on the table. The tag on her uniform said her name was Ashley, and she wasn't much older than me. Her hair was blond, almost the exact shade mine had been when we were in Playa Hermosa. Her face was bright and open, the face of someone who'd never had to hide anything important. I wondered about her. Was she working her way through college? Saving for a gap year? What would it be like to have a life where you could wake up with your own name? Where you didn't have to look over your shoulder all the time?

"Can I get you anything else?" she asked.

"No, thanks."

I devoured the eggs, bacon, and toast before pulling the plate of pancakes toward me. Then I opened my notebook and shoveled bites into my mouth while I studied the blank page, my mind turning over the possibilities. It didn't take me long to realize the list of things I could to do help Parker was short: I could break him out of jail or I could turn myself in.

Breaking him out of jail was basically out of the question. I might as well just turn myself in and save everyone the trouble, because there was no way I could get someone out of the LA County Jail system. And even if I could, it would take time and planning. A lot of time and planning. I would need resources way beyond the ones I had. At some point, Parker would go to trial. After that, my chance to help him would be gone, and I couldn't let that happen. Parker wouldn't survive a long sentence. Not because he wasn't tough; he was one of the toughest people I'd ever met. But he had a wild heart. Even with Cormac and Renee, Parker would slink off into the dark, disappearing for hours and sometimes even days without a word. Being in a cage would kill him.

Which brought me back to turning myself in. Could I trade myself for Parker? Would they go easier on him if I stepped forward and corroborated his story, that he and I had been adopted by Cormac and Renee to further their cons? That we'd had little choice but to follow the lead of the only parents we had? They were truths I'd avoided for a long time, but that time was past. I had to be honest now—starting with myself—because I was finally beginning to understand that those were the most dangerous lies of all.

Would an attorney be able to tell me if turning myself in was an option? I was pretty sure they couldn't rat me out if I paid them something. Then I would be their client, and they were obligated by law to keep the confidence of a client. At least, I thought that was how it worked.

I did some quick math on the next page of my notebook. I

still had a little over twenty-four hundred dollars. It sounded like a lot, but at a hundred and twenty dollars a night, the hotel would eat through my money fast, and that wasn't counting the cost of food and transportation. At my current spending rate, I guessed I had enough money for a couple of weeks. I might be able to find a slightly cheaper hotel, but nothing was really cheap in the neighborhoods surrounding Playa Hermosa, and a less expensive hotel would buy me an extra week or two at most. I didn't know how long it would take to help Parker, but I was pretty sure it would be longer than that.

I poured myself another cup of coffee and toyed with the possibility of renting a room or studio apartment. I quickly discarded the idea. By the time I paid first and last months' rent, plus a security deposit—something I knew was required from all the places Cormac and Renee had rented for us—it would be a wash. Definitely not worth the extra exposure.

I watched as Ashley came back and cleared the dishes from the table. I could get a job. Maybe. But then I'd need a new Social Security card and ID, both of which would take time and connections. And there was the exposure problem again. Bosses and coworkers and customers. No good.

I'd known I was going into my rescue mission unprepared, but I'd expected to have more money at least. More money meant more time to figure things out. Now I was short on both.

"Can I get you some fresh coffee?" Ashley asked.

I shook my head. "Just the check, thanks."

She reached into the apron at her waist and withdrew my ticket. "Have a great day."

"You too," I said. I wondered what she would do after her shift. Go to the gym? Meet up with friends at the beach?

I paid the check and headed for a Rite Aid two blocks down. It was almost noon, but the temperature was mild, the sun hiding behind the marine layer blowing in off the beach. The coastal eddy, I think they called it. Selena had once told me that it didn't get really hot and sunny in the South Bay until late July. Before then, a heavy layer of clouds rolled in off the ocean, draping itself over the area like a soggy blanket. It kept the temperatures mild and sometimes even cool, the antithesis of the stereotypical Southern California climate.

I forced myself to be vigilant as I walked, watching for signs that I'd been made: nondescript cars with more than one person hiding behind sunglasses or a newspaper, windowless vans that could be hiding surveillance equipment, an unusual number of clean-cut guys in an area known for hippies and surfers. But everything was cool, the sidewalks basically empty. This was the Southern California suburbs; no one walked anywhere when they could drive instead.

At Rite Aid I picked up the stuff from my list and started back for the hotel. I entered through the front doors first and took the elevator up, but instead of stopping at the door to my room, I continued on to the stairwell, wanting to make sure no one was waiting there. I'd heard too many of Cormac's raid stories—accounts of fellow grifters who'd been caught—to be careless so close to Playa Hermosa. According to Cormac, SWAT teams hid on fire escapes and in adjoining apartments, in stairwells and in work vans. Sometimes someone would come to the door disguised as a delivery person, asking for a signature to make sure they got the right person before the rest of the team swooped in. Other times a group of them would come in full force so the suspect wouldn't have time to plan an escape.

I took the stairs to the first floor, confirmed that the stairwell was empty, and headed back upstairs to let myself into the room. Housekeeping had come while I was gone, and the room looked exactly like it had when I'd checked in two days before.

I put my backpack down on the bed and set my laptop up on the little table by the window. I used my new prepaid credit card to access the Wi-Fi for the next twenty-four hours, then signed up for an account on a VPN to mask my activity.

I started by looking up attorney-client privilege. According to Wikipedia, privilege existed as long as the communication happens between a client and his or her attorney for the sake of securing legal advice. I read through the list of exceptions, my gaze snagging on the third one: *the communication is made for the purpose of committing a crime.* I wasn't planning to commit a crime. Was I? Did it count that I was willing to do anything to get Parker out of jail? What if I talked to the attorney and then decided that committing another crime was the only way to do it? Would the possible logistics of my situation—like getting a new fake ID—count as committing a crime?

I didn't know, and I wasn't willing to risk finding out. I filed the option away for later consideration and went back over the newspaper articles about the Fairchild con and Parker's arrest.

I typed the name of Parker's attorney into the search bar, then clicked Images. A severe-looking woman blossomed in several photographs across the screen. Her face was smooth and unlined, her red hair pulled back into a tight bun. Once I had a picture of her in my mind, I searched for information about her other cases, hoping she had experience with at least one high-profile case like Parker's. But the closest she'd come was a robbery gone bad in Hawthorne. The suspect had been seventeen and coerced into the theft by his older brother, a well-known gangbanger. The younger brother was convicted as an adult and sentenced to ten years for accessory to murder. Not exactly promising.

I read through articles on the Fairchild theft chronologically, starting with the ones that appeared right after we'd stolen the gold. There were stock photos of Warren, commanding in a suit and tie, obviously some kind of promotional photo for the billion-dollar company owned by his father. The picture held no trace of the Warren I knew, the mentally ill man who'd stockpiled gold in a bunker under his carriage house, security against an unknown threat that only he saw coming. There were a few pictures of Parker, too, and my heart leaped into my throat at the defiant lift of his chin, the stubborn shine in his eyes. His face was more familiar to me than my own, and I suddenly missed him with a force that almost brought me to my knees.

I clicked on more of the results, skimming the articles for something, anything, I could use.

. . . Detective Castillo said the investigation is ongoing.

A press release issued by lead detective Raul Castillo claimed that . . .

. . . questions into the investigation, led by Detective Castillo . . .

It didn't sound like they had much. Parker wasn't talking. I knew it was because of me. He didn't care about the grifter code. If he could have sold Cormac and Renee down the river to save himself, he would have. And I didn't blame him. But he knew I'd gotten away, and he had no idea what had happened with Renee. He probably thought I was still with her and Cormac, and he would never do anything to put me in danger.

My stomach twisted. I needed to get word to him that I was in town. That I was going to help him. But first I needed to figure out what to do.

I looked at the name on my screen. Raul Castillo.

Five

I took a bus to the Galleria later that afternoon. There was another mall that was closer, but I wanted to get as far away as possible from the hotel. I knew the cops couldn't track the disposable phone to me through an account, but I didn't know if they could track its location. I was covering my bases, just in case.

When I got to the mall, I took the elevator to the roof of the parking garage to make sure I had a solid signal. I reached into my pocket and pulled out the piece of paper where I'd written the phone number. Then I dialed.

"Good afternoon. You have reached the Playa Hermosa Police Department." A recorded voice filled my ear. "If this is an emergency, please hang up and dial nine-one-one. Please listen carefully, as our menu options have changed. If you know your party's extension, you may dial it at any time.

If you know the name of your party, please press one now."

I took the phone away from my ear and pressed the 1 key.

I followed the directions to enter the first three letters of Raul Castillo's last name. A moment later I heard a soft click, followed by a tinny electronic voice:

"Raul Castillo, extension four-twenty-three."

I made a mental note of the extension number as the phone started to ring. A few seconds later, a purposeful male voice spoke.

"You have reached voice mail for Raul Castillo, detective with the Playa Hermosa Police Department. Please leave your name and number, and I'll return your call."

I was frozen by the beep. Seconds ticked by in silence before I finally spoke, afraid the voice mail would disconnect without some kind of noise indicating I was still on the line.

"Uh . . . this is . . . this is Grace Fontaine. I want to talk about Parker. Parker Fontaine." I hesitated, then finished in a rush, worried about staying on the line too long. "I'll call you back."

I disconnected the call, my heart bumping against my chest like a wild bird in a cage. I took a few deep breaths, trying to calm myself down enough to figure out what was next. I had been stupid to think Detective Castillo would pick up on my first try. Everyone had voice mail, and cops probably weren't at their desks a whole lot, especially cops investigating a high-profile crime like the Fairchild theft.

It was after four in the afternoon, but detectives

sometimes worked late, didn't they? And maybe it would be better to catch Raul Castillo when most of the people in his office were gone. Would he wait for my call when he got my message? Would he even get it tonight?

I finally headed into the mall. I wasn't anxious to go back to the four walls of my hotel room, the taupe paint and bad art a reminder that it was temporary shelter, that I'd have to find another place to stay soon.

I wandered around for an hour, looking in the windows of the stores Selena and I had visited together, remembering how it had felt to have a friend, to laugh about clothes and guys and forget myself for just a little while. At the time, it had felt unexplainably like a beginning. Like the mistakes of my past had been wiped clean and I was finally getting a chance to start over. That's what people say when you're young, isn't it? That it's okay to make mistakes, that you can afford to make them because there's always time to set things right?

I knew now that it was a romantic notion, one that was only true for certain kinds of people. People who had a store-house of opportunity like a cat that has nine lives. People who hadn't made mistakes that were so big, there was no coming back from them.

When I'd circled the mall twice, I stopped at the food court and got a plate of greasy Chinese food. I ate it at a table on the edge of the crowd, watching people come and go. When I was finished, I dumped my trash, careful not to look at anyone too long or too hard.

It was almost six thirty when I headed back to the parking garage. I took the stairs to the top again and pulled out my phone. I'd give Raul Castillo one more try tonight. If he didn't answer, I'd go back to the hotel and try again tomorrow.

I dialed the number for the Playa Hermosa Police Department, but this time I entered Raul Castillo's extension number. I was preparing to leave another message when a voice filled my ear.

"Raul Castillo."

There was expectation in it, and I knew he'd been waiting for me.

"It's Grace Fontaine."

He exhaled. "Grace, I'm so glad you called back. Where are you?"

"I'm not ready to tell you that yet," I said. "I want to talk about Parker."

"Okay, let's talk."

"I want . . ." I stumbled a little. I wanted Parker to be free, to be let go, but I wasn't naive enough to believe just asking for it would make it happen. "What happened wasn't his fault. I want to help him."

"That's a tough one, Grace." I thought I heard genuine kindness in his voice, although it could have been an act. He was a detective. They were probably trained to get people to turn themselves in or give themselves away. "Crimes have been committed. Someone has died. Parker is the only one here to take the fall."

I glanced at my phone, wanting to keep track of how long I was on the line so I could disconnect the call before too much time had passed. It had been forty-five seconds.

"That's not his fault. He's just a kid like me."

"Not a kid." I could almost hear Detective Castillo shaking his head. "Parker's eighteen. Even you're not considered a kid by the justice system. Not if you're seventeen or older."

My stomach clutched a little at his words. I'd celebrated my seventeenth birthday in Bellevue, with a gourmet strawberry cake from Miranda's favorite bakery and a Tiffany bracelet, probably bought with Miranda's money, from her and Cormac. Miranda had thought I was turning eighteen.

"We were forced to do what we did. We had no choice." Saying the words out loud for the first time did something to me. Made my voice crack, my throat fill with thick and tangled tears.

"I have no doubt that's true, Grace. Why don't you come in so we can talk about it?" He hesitated, and when he spoke again, his voice was gentle. "Are you all alone?"

I looked at the phone. One minute and thirty-two seconds. I thought I remembered Cormac saying that it took the police two minutes to trace a call, but I couldn't be sure.

"I have to go," I said.

"Listen to me, Grace." His voice was a rush of wind into the phone. Then he spoke lower, softer. "I can help you, but things are getting complicated here. There's not much time."

One minute forty-one seconds.

"I have to go."

"Meet me somewhere," he said hurriedly, trying to get the words in before I hung up. "Anywhere. Just you and me. We'll figure out a way to help Parker."

One minute forty-eight seconds.

"I'll call you back."

I hung up, my chest rising and falling, breath coming fast and hard, like I'd been running.

Six

I spent the night eating takeout in my underwear while my clothes, washed in the bathtub, dried on hangers around the room. I stared at the TV while I ate, letting the images flash in front of my eyes as I replayed Detective Castillo's words. He'd sounded sincere, like he really cared and wanted to help.

Are you all alone?

I was. More alone than I'd ever been, and that was saying something.

I finally turned off the TV and fell into a dream-filled sleep.

Logan floated in the ocean next to me, our bodies rising and falling with the swell of the tide. We held hands, our entwined fingers buoyant on the briny water. I felt his hand slip from mine, but when I looked over at him, his face morphed into Parker's. He sank slowly below the surface, still on his back, the pale flash of his skin growing dimmer as I reached for him. I ducked under the water and opened my eyes, but instead of Parker, I saw a flash of gold underneath me: the gold bars we'd stolen from Warren Fairchild, stacked on the sandy ocean floor. I looked frantically around, but Parker was nowhere to be found. I was starting to swim for the surface, my breath swelling in my lungs, clamoring for release, when something grabbed me. I looked down, a cry of protest arising in a stream of bubbles from my mouth as I saw a dark-haired woman, her face gray and bloated, her fingers wrapped tightly around my arm.

It was after ten o'clock in the morning when I woke up sweating, clutching my throat and gasping for air like I'd been holding my breath. I took a shower and brushed my teeth, still shaken from the nightmare. After I got dressed, I opened the curtains. I was hoping the California sun would banish the residual dread in my veins, but I was greeted with a bank of gunmetal clouds that almost completely blotted out the light. Rain beaded the window, the ocean lost to fog in the distance. I wondered if Logan and the others had been surfing. He always said some of the best swells came in just before a storm.

The thought brought forward a flash of memory: Logan emerging from the water with his surfboard as the sun hung over the horizon. I was sitting on a blanket, trying to focus on my book when all I really wanted to do was look at him. He'd shaken his wet hair over me, causing me to shriek in protest, and he'd laughed as he peeled off his wet suit. After that, we'd huddled under a blanket, kissing and touching and talking, until the sun went down on the deserted beach. His skin had been cold and smooth. He'd smelled like the sea.

I took a shower and spent an hour in front of the mirror using makeup to sculpt a different face. I made my eyes look smaller by rimming them with black liner all the way around, then swept dark blush into the hollows of my cheekbones to make my face appear even gaunter than it already was. Subtle shading along either side of my nose made it look longer and more narrow, and nude gloss took the attention off my lips. By the time I was finished, I didn't look at all like Grace Fontaine. I didn't look like Julie Montrose either. I stared at the stranger in the mirror and felt completely unattached to the reflection.

I paid for another day at the hotel on my way out. If I didn't find a solution soon, I'd have to move. Budget hotels were havens for transients: businesspeople, travelers on their way someplace else, families stopping for the night during a road trip. I'd already been there four days. I was going to draw attention to myself if I didn't move soon.

I stopped at Denny's for breakfast, then walked to the corner of Hawthorne and Pacific Coast Highway and caught the bus. My pulse quickened as we made our way up the winding hills of the peninsula, the bus's engine straining against the incline. The light was already dim and gray, but once we hit Cove Road, it grew even darker, the thick net of foliage overhead blocking out what little light made it through the clouds.

I remembered the first time I'd seen Playa Hermosa, the

way it had felt like a tropical jungle, like I was leaving reality behind for someplace warm and magical, removed from all of life's ugly realities. Maybe it was just the weather, but this time felt different, like I was swimming into an underwater cave, hoping for an exit on the other side but knowing deep down I would be met with a wall of rock.

The bus slowly emptied out as we climbed the winding roads. By the time we stopped at the Town Center, the bus's last stop before heading back to Torrance, I was the only one left. I wasn't surprised. Who took the bus to Playa Hermosa? The people who lived here had multiple vehicles in their driveways, usually expensive European sports cars, luxury sedans, and high-end SUVs, plenty to go around for the parents and their kids, gifted with brand-new models on their sixteenth birthdays.

I got off the bus and immediately started walking, making a point to avoid Mike's. Other than the Cove, it was the most likely spot for Logan and the others to hang out. School didn't let out for an hour, but it was the end of senior year for most of them, and I couldn't be sure they were all on a normal schedule. I imagined them there, clustered around the big red booth in the back, laughing and eating cheese fries. Rachel would be playing tic-tac-toe on the back of a menu with Harper while Liam entertained everyone with his latest exploits in the water. Would Logan be there, too? Or did his carefree days with the group end the night we took his father's gold?

I pushed the thought away. I couldn't do anything about

that. I was here for Parker. He was the one I could still help, the one who was counting on me. I didn't know if I could live with the damage I'd done to Logan and his family, but for now I would live for Parker. I would put one foot in front of the other to right the only wrong I had any control over. I would have to figure out what I could and couldn't live with later, after Parker was free.

I turned off the main road as soon as I could. Playa Hermosa's residential neighborhoods were connected to the rest of the South Bay by one main artery, and I didn't want to be seen by anyone who might be driving by. I knew I looked different on the outside, but it was hard to believe my crime wasn't emblazoned on my face, visible to everyone.

Above the Town Center, Playa Hermosa was nothing but a series of twisty, steeply inclined roads. My legs burned as I climbed, and I was suddenly grateful for the cloud cover that kept the sun from burning too hot on my head. I felt the tug of melancholy as I walked, the breeze salty and familiar, the smell of wild jasmine permeating the air. Bougainvillea climbed across stone walls and trellises, over fences and up the sides of houses. Somewhere in the trees I heard the caw of the wild parrots that made their home here. It made me think of the man who had lived next door on Camino Jardin, the old music he liked to hum, his voice calling out to the birds in the trees.

I wondered how the peacocks were faring, if the residents of Playa Hermosa had won their battle to have them removed because of the noise and their penchant for standing in the middle of the road. I thought with a pang of sadness of the one Cormac had run over after the Fairchild con. Another casualty of all our lies.

It took me twenty minutes to reach Selena's neighborhood and another fifteen to find a good place to hide. The street was fronted by houses on both sides, the road clear except for an empty blue Range Rover at the curb. Not exactly overflowing with possibilities. I finally tucked myself into the nook created by a small arbor in front of the house across the street from Selena's. It didn't have a garage—a lot of the older houses in Playa Hermosa didn't—and there were no cars in the driveway. I guessed it was empty, and I felt relatively certain the bougainvillea growing up the sides of the arbor would conceal me from a casual observer.

I'd been there about a half hour when a fine mist started to fall from the sky. I pulled the hood up on my jacket and tucked myself farther back into the arbor, keeping my eyes on the small stucco house that belonged to Selena and the father who'd raised her. I flashed back to my dream, to the woman underwater. I had somehow known she was Selena's mother even though she'd been long gone by the time we came to Playa Hermosa. I was contemplating the subconscious meaning of her appearance in my nightmare when I saw a flash of red on the sidewalk across the street.

I squinted, trying to focus through the water netting the air. A lone figure walked down the sidewalk. The person was almost completely obscured by a red raincoat, but I would have known it was Selena even without the strand of curly dark hair that escaped from the hood. It was something in the way she walked, body leaning forward like she always had somewhere important to be, gaze focused like she was so far inside her own head that she wasn't aware of the world around her. Until she looked at you. Then there was never any doubt that she was really there.

I watched her hurry toward the walkway leading to the house across the street. She was alone, and I wondered what had happened to Nina, the girl who'd walked home with Selena before I'd pulled her into Logan's crowd. Selena hadn't had a lot of friends, but the ones she had were consistent, people she could eat lunch with every day or walk home from school with. Had they turned on her because of her association with me? I could hardly stand to think about it.

I took a step forward as she turned onto the landscaped path leading to her house. I needed to talk to her. We'd been friends first, before I'd been accepted into Logan's group. I don't know why that made me think she might give me a chance to make things right. Maybe because it was the only hope I had.

But I couldn't make my feet move, and I stood helplessly by as she stepped onto the stone porch. She put a hand into her bag, then reached for the door. It swung open, and a minute later she disappeared behind it, as lost to me as I'd been to her when we left Playa Hermosa the night everything had gone so wrong.

Seven

I walked back to the Town Center, the rain falling harder and more insistently. The sky had turned a darker shade of gray, and somewhere in the distance I thought I heard the low rumble of thunder. I felt closed in and cut off by the rain, by the hood pulled up around my face, by my isolation.

I stood back in the Plexiglas shelter while I waited for the bus. I knew I was hardly visible from the street, but I still felt exposed, and I was relieved when the bus finally pulled up in a cloud of exhaust and a screech of brakes.

I looked out the window, thinking about Selena as we wound our way down the peninsula. I should have approached her. Asking her for help was the only option I had. Waiting wasn't going to change that, and it wasn't going to make talking to her easier, either. Nothing would do that. I didn't want to talk to her, not just because it was a risk to my freedom—and by extension Parker's—but because she didn't deserve it. Didn't deserve to be pulled back into the mess I'd made. It was just another way of victimizing her, of punishing her for caring about me.

I ran through all the other possibilities, returning to Detective Castillo. I didn't think Selena would call the cops, but I couldn't be sure. Detective Castillo could tell me if turning myself in would help Parker. If it would, I'd do it today, and I wouldn't need to approach Selena at all. If it wouldn't, I'd be back at square one. But it was worth a shot.

I rode the bus past my stop, all the way down the Pacific Coast Highway into Lomita, a mean-looking city close to the San Pedro waterfront. It was hard to believe Playa Hermosa was less than twenty minutes away; Lomita was paved and sidewalked to within an inch of its life, the lush greenery of the peninsula nothing but a memory in the shadow of countless crumbling stucco apartment buildings. I would have preferred the opposite direction and the beach, but I didn't want the sound of the water to give away my location.

I got off the bus at a fast-food stand on the corner. My stomach was scooped out with hunger, but there was no way I could think about food until I did what I had to do.

I walked around back, pulling Detective Castillo's number from my pocket. I stared down at the numbers, racking my brain for another way. There wasn't one, and I took out my cell phone and dialed before I could talk myself into postponing the inevitable.

I waited for the automated greeting, then punched in

Detective Castillo's extension. It only rang twice before I heard his voice on the other end of the phone.

"Detective Castillo."

I didn't bother with a greeting. The clock was already ticking. "It's Grace Fontaine."

"Grace." He breathed my name into the phone, and I wondered if I was imagining the relief in his voice. Had he been waiting for me to call? "Are you all right?"

It took me by surprise. I couldn't remember the last time someone had asked me that question. "I'm . . . I'm fine," I said. "I want to talk about Parker."

"Okay," he said.

"What happened isn't his fault. He didn't kill that guard."

"I know that, Grace. The evidence doesn't match up. But he was part of the Fairchild theft, and I'm guessing you were too."

I hesitated, trying to think of a way to impart as much information as possible in the short amount of time before I would have to disconnect the call. "We didn't plan any of it. We were both kids. We did what we were told by the people taking care of us."

"I hear you, Grace, but Parker's eighteen." I heard a note of regret in his voice. "He's considered responsible for his actions, and so are you. Unless . . ."

I seized on the word. "Unless?"

"If you could get us information about the people who were really behind it, you might be able to cut a deal with the prosecutor."

"What kind of information?"

There was silence on the other end of the line before he finally spoke again. "That's a complicated question. Why don't we meet and talk about it? Just you and me."

I looked at the call time on my phone. One minute thirty-one seconds.

"I . . . I don't know," I said, running possible scenarios through my mind. Would he bring backup to a meeting with me? Was it a trick so he could throw me in jail with Parker?

"I want to help you, Grace. I do. But listen . . ." I heard the squeak of his desk chair followed by footsteps. When he spoke again, his voice was muffled, like he was trying to be quiet. "Things are happening here that will impact the case. I might not be able to help you much longer."

"What kind of things?"

He was so quiet that I wondered if he'd heard the question. "I'll fill you in when we meet," he finally said.

"I don't know . . ."

"Come on, Grace. You need help here. You know it, and I know it. Let me help you."

One minute fifty seconds.

"I have to go," I said. "I'll call you back in an hour."

I disconnected the call and leaned against the stained exterior of the building. My chest felt tight, and it was suddenly hard to breathe. I swayed a little, my head buzzing. The last thing I needed was to pass out in public a few miles from Playa Hermosa.

I stood there for a minute, forcing myself to take slow,

deep breaths until my head cleared. When I felt almost normal, I went inside and ordered a cheeseburger and fries to go, then waited for the next bus heading back to Torrance.

I took a seat in the back and ate the burger while the city passed by on the other side of the dirty glass. I heard Detective Castillo's voice in my head: *You need help here. You know it, and I know it.*

He was right. My money was dwindling fast, something that wouldn't change as long as I was on the run. I could follow through on my original plan to ask Selena for help, but all roads still led back to Detective Castillo. Regardless of where I slept, I'd need to talk to him eventually, figure out if I could trade information on Cormac and Renee for Parker's freedom. And what had he meant about things changing? Did they have a break in the case? Something they were going to announce soon?

I looked at my watch. It had been forty-two minutes since I'd hung up with Detective Castillo. I got off the bus at the corner of PCH and Hawthorne and started walking. At the one-hour mark, I called him again.

"Grace." He picked it up even before I heard it ring. "I'm not tracing this call. You don't have to hurry off the phone every time we talk."

"The Reel Inn at the Third Street Promenade, tomorrow at one p.m.," I said. "And give me your cell phone number."

I wrote the number in my notebook as he recited it over the phone. "I'll be there, Grace. And I'll come alone."

Eight

The surfers were just climbing out of the water when I reached Santa Monica early the next morning. I got off the bus and walked toward the promenade, my footsteps heavy and sluggish. I'd slept soundly and without nightmares, but I was dragging, a deep-seated exhaustion taking root in my bones. I'd been on the move almost constantly, taking the bus from one end of town to the other, walking to Selena's house, to out-of-the-way places to call Detective Castillo. It was wearing on me, and I knew I'd need to find a way to regroup before I lost focus and started making mistakes.

I took a deep breath, sucking in the ocean air, trying to keep myself alert. The sun glinted off the Ferris wheel on the pier, and I had a sudden flash of Logan's face, inches from mine as we rose over the ocean in one of the tin buckets, his arm securely around my shoulders, the feeling that nothing in the world could come between us as long as we kept climbing into the sky. It hurt to remember, a physical ache in my chest, like my heart had been scraped out, the wound left empty and rotting.

I continued toward the Reel Inn. Logan had taken me there for dinner the night we'd come to the promenade, and while I didn't plan to use it as a meeting spot for Detective Castillo, it was a good place to start the scavenger hunt that would lead him to me.

The restaurant stood on a corner at the end of the promenade. I walked slowly past it, not wanting to draw attention to myself, casing the surrounding businesses. There was a children's boutique on one side and a specialty paper store on the other. Across from it stood a bookstore, and next to that a café and coffee shop. I made note of it all and looked up, scanning the rooftops for places the cops might hide to watch my meeting with Detective Castillo.

Once I had a handle on the area around the Reel Inn, I continued along the promenade, looking for places to send Detective Castillo while I watched to make sure he wasn't being followed. Finally, I chose the place that would be our last stop: a P.F. Chang's that was close to a parking garage and a bunch of stores that could provide hiding spots if I needed them. I'd been to a P.F. Chang's in Seattle, and I knew the lighting was dim, the furnishings dark. It was nearly always crowded, and the kitchen would give me an alternate way out if things went bad. Small things might vary from location to location, but chain restaurants were always

designed to look and feel the same to the people who frequented them. I was willing to bet this one was almost iden-
tical to the one in Seattle. At one p.m., the place would be
packed.

Recon complete, I bought a breakfast burrito and a coffee from one of the hole-in-the-wall food places close to the
beach. I'd planned to avoid the water, but I felt the pull of it
like the tide to the moon, and I found myself heading for the
pier and taking the stairs down to the still-cool sand almost
without thinking.

I sat down near the water. The beach was deserted except
for a few surfers, rising and falling on the waves, and the
joggers that populated every beach I'd ever been to in California. Gulls wheeled out over the sea, calling to one another
as they swooped down, skimming fish and scraps of food
off the surface. The water crawled toward my feet before
withdrawing back into the well of the ocean. The sound of
it was hypnotic, and my nerves smoothed out just a little. I
closed my eyes, letting my breath match the rhythm of it,
trying to commit the sound and smell to memory. Maybe I
could call on it the next time I was heaving against a crumbling building, trying to catch my breath.

By the time I finished my breakfast, I felt a little better.
More in control. Like I might actually be able to pull it all
off. I made my way back up to the promenade and bought a
bottled water at the café across the street from the Reel Inn.
Then I sat down at one of the window seats and waited.

I wasn't due to meet Detective Castillo for nearly two
hours, but if the police were setting up a sting, they'd have

to do it in advance. I pulled out a magazine I'd pilfered from the lobby of the hotel and scanned the surrounding buildings through the lenses of my aviators. I looked for sudden movement around the restaurant, for a group of people—mostly men—moving toward it. I looked for activity on the roof, people talking on headsets, meaningful glances that would be out of place passed between strangers. But it was quiet.

The crowd slowly increased as the lunch hour approached. People walked by with shopping bags and paper cups of coffee. There were even a few uniformed officers strolling the walkway. But no one was in a hurry. No one was being too careful, too casual.

Thirty minutes before I was scheduled to meet Detective Castillo, little had changed. Someone had opened the door to the Reel Inn, propping it open with a sandwich board, and there were a few more people, some of them in business suits, hurrying over the walkway. But that was it. No police that I could see and nothing that could be an undercover operation. If Detective Castillo's men were moving in, they were completely undetectable to my eyes.

I'd found only a couple of photos online of Raul Castillo, both of them taken during press conferences. In one shot he was standing off to the side, hands clasped behind his back, eyes aimed at someone in a suit standing in front of a microphone. In the second picture he'd been half hidden behind a detective named Fletcher, whose steely gaze was aimed directly at the camera. Neither of the angles had provided me with a full view of Detective Castillo's face. Instead I had gotten a glimpse of powerful shoulders, a strong jaw beneath unsmiling eyes, dark hair cut close to the head. I kept the images in mind as I watched the front door of the Reel Inn, afraid to even blink in case I missed him.

Finally, just before one p.m., a solidly built man approached the restaurant. He moved so quickly and with such assurance that I almost dismissed him. I'd expected him to look around, to try to spot me before he went inside. But he moved toward the door with single-minded purpose. He was wearing a navy Windbreaker, his eyes hidden behind aviators that weren't very different from the cheap ones I'd bought at Rite Aid. I wondered if he had been in the military; he had that kind of gait, confident that nothing would deter him from his purpose, daring anything—or anyone—to try.

I took out my phone and dialed as he disappeared inside the restaurant.

"Grace?"

"Leave the restaurant and turn left. Keep walking until you get to the Gap. Go inside, all the way to the back of the store."

"You don't have to—"

I hung up before he could finish. A few seconds later he appeared in front of the restaurant and started walking. I waited, watching for signs of anyone on the move, anyone following him. There weren't any, and I stood up and left the café.

I hung back, careful to keep the navy Windbreaker in

view as it bobbed in and out of the growing lunchtime crowd. My heart was beating a mile a minute, and a bead of sweat dripped down my back. I half expected to hear the clatter of boots behind me, the voice of someone telling me to freeze. When he ducked into the Gap, I stopped at a hat kiosk in the middle of the promenade and dialed his number while I tried on fedoras and newsboys.

He sighed in lieu of a greeting. "I came alone. Like I said I would."

"Great. Leave the Gap and walk to the corner. Turn right and keep walking until you hit P.F. Chang's. Go inside and sit at the bar with your back to the door." I disconnected the call and put my phone in my pocket.

He appeared a moment later. I watched him follow my instructions; then I returned the sun hat I'd been trying on and moved into the crowd.

I tailed him to P.F. Chang's, still hanging back. He worked his way around a group of people in business suits, skirts, and button-downs and disappeared inside the restaurant. I waited two minutes before I went inside.

The restaurant was as dark as I remembered, and I stood in the entryway, letting my eyes adjust to the dim lighting. I looked through the people standing around—talking about work, texting, waiting for a table—until I found the bar.

He was sitting there, his broad back to the door just liked I'd instructed.

I took one last glance around. Nothing seemed out of the ordinary, and I started for the bar, marking the swinging kitchen doors in case I needed a quick escape.

Time seemed to slow down. I waited for a hand on my arm, a shout through the crowd, a group of uniformed men to appear from the kitchen or the hallway leading to the bathrooms. No way would Detective Castillo let go of an opportunity to bring me in. Not on a high-profile case attached to a name like Warren Fairchild. It would be a career maker— or a career breaker.

Detective Castillo's navy-clad back remained in front of me. Once I reached him, detaining me would be as simple as a cuff around my wrist, a tight hold on my arm. I wasn't some kind of highly trained assassin. I knew people, not martial arts. If he wanted to take me in, even by himself, there wouldn't be much I could do to stop him.

I slid carefully into the seat next to him, surprised to see that he seemed to be reading the menu.

"I made you back at the Reel Inn." He turned to face me. "But I said I'd come alone, and I did."

Nine

He insisted we order lunch, and I shoveled spicy dan dan noodles into my mouth, slowly at first in case it was an attempt to distract me while his men moved in, and then more quickly when I realized he was really alone.

"How is Parker?" I finally asked Detective Castillo.

He wiped his mouth on his napkin and took a long drink of water. "I haven't seen him since he was moved to County. No point."

"What do you mean?"

He shrugged a little, the gesture incongruous coming from such a big guy. "He wasn't going to crack. Knew that right away. I've seen grown men, hard men, who are less calm when their balls—" His cheeks reddened. "Sorry. When they're up against a wall."

I nodded. "Not much scares Parker. But also, he didn't

really know where we were going. Neither did I."

Detective Castillo raised his eyebrows. "Mom and Dad keep those details to themselves, huh?"

Now it was my turn to blush. A second later, anger rose behind my embarrassment. "It worked, didn't it? Parker couldn't tell you anything because he didn't know anything."

He leaned in. "Worked for them. Parker's in jail, and you're trying to negotiate his freedom with information I don't think you have."

I swallowed hard, my bluster gone. "I know all about them," I said, a little desperate. "How they set things up, what they look for."

"Do you know where they are now?" he asked.

"Cormac was in Washington State when I last saw him."

"When was that?"

I thought about it. "A week ago?"

He nodded. "And Renee?"

I looked down, trying to ignore the sucker punch I felt to my gut every time someone mentioned the only mother I'd ever really known. I couldn't think about her, couldn't hear her name without remembering how I'd felt that day in the hotel room when Cormac and I had discovered her betrayal. I'd had five months to get past the hurt and anger. Now I was just ashamed. Ashamed of being naive enough to believe she'd really loved me.

"She left right after the Fairchild job," I finally said. "With the gold."

He sighed, drumming his fingers on the top of the bar.

"What can you tell us about their operation? Do you have contacts? People who gave you fake IDs, provided you with financial information, that kind of thing?"

I combed through our jobs in my mind, already knowing it was pointless. Cormac and Renee had kept Parker and me insulated from the details. They'd said it was for our own good, but I was starting to realize they were the only ones who'd benefited from the arrangement.

I finally shook my head. "They didn't tell us that kind of stuff. Cormac planned everything. He only told us what we needed to know to get the job done." I paused. "What about the details of the Fairchild job? I could tell you about that: how we planned it, how Cormac came back from Allied with blood on his shirt . . ."

He sat up a little straighter. "Were you there when the altercation with the guard happened?"

"No, but I saw the blood, and Cormac said they did what they had to do. Or maybe that was Renee. . . ." I thought back to that final, terrifying night at the Fairchilds' when everything had come crashing down around us. "I think it was Renee."

Detective Castillo rubbed his chin. "It's not enough. Parker was part of a major robbery—and so were you, I might add. Someone died. They could take my badge for having this conversation instead of bringing you in. I know you're the best chance we have for nailing the people responsible, and I want to help you, but if you want to help Parker, you're going to need real information: where they get their fake documents, who's part of the underground network that supports them, where they get private data on their marks. None of those things are easy to come by. My hunch is that they have some heavy hitters on the payroll. That kind of information would be worth a trade to the prosecutor."

"I don't know any of that stuff." I heard the defeat in my own voice.

He sighed. "I hate to say it, but that's not our only problem."

"What do you mean?"

"They've put another detective on the case."

I sat up straighter. "You mean you're not even working it anymore?" I fought against a surge of hysteria. "Then what am I doing here?"

His eyes scanned the restaurant, like he was as afraid of being seen as I was, then spoke more softly. "I'm still on the case, but the chief has partnered me up with some ass—" He cleared his throat. "With another detective from LA County."

"What does that mean for Parker? For me?" I asked.

"It means we have to hurry. Fletcher is an attack dog looking for his next piece of steak."

I had a flash of the flinty-eyed man blocking Detective Castillo in the photograph I'd found online. Fletcher. "What are you saying exactly?"

He seemed to think about what he would say next. "Word on the street is Fletcher's not as interested in the truth as he is in his next promotion, and he's all but guaranteed one if he can bring in you or Cormac or Renee. He's been all over the case files, reinterviewing people, rescouting the scene of the crime . . . The DA wants this case solved, Grace. His campaign contributors aren't too happy with the idea of people cozying up to their sons and daughters and then stealing from them right under their noses."

My cheeks burned.

"Sorry," he said.

"It's okay," I said softly. "It's the truth."

He seemed to hesitate. "I feel obligated to tell you that you should turn yourself in, to remind you that you're a fugitive from the law and that the best thing to do is to throw yourself on the mercy of the court."

"You don't sound convinced," I said.

"Once you're in custody, you won't have access to any of the information that might be a bargaining chip for Parker— or for yourself. That's a fact." He sighed again, his shoulders sagging a little. "I just hate to see you become collateral damage if there's a chance to do it another way."

"So what should I do?"

He was drumming again, his fingertips rising and falling on the bar. "I'll tell you what—I'll call in a favor in Seattle, see if anyone can get a line on Cormac. If he's still there, the tip should give you at least a little leverage with the prosecutor."

"And if he's not?"

"I don't know. Let me run down this lead, see where it takes me." I gave him the alias Cormac was using and he wrote it in a notebook he pulled from his jacket pocket. "In the meantime, you should think through everything you've done with Cormac and Renee. Every job, every detail. Did you wait in the car while one of them talked to a source? Were you ever with them when they picked up your documents? Did they let slip the name of someone feeding them financial information on your marks? Even something small could lead us to something big, so don't discount anything." He reached into his pocket. "Let me take your number and I'll call you in a couple of days."

I shook my head. "I'm not giving you my number. I'll get in touch with you in two days."

There was something sad in his eyes as he nodded. "Call me any time of the day or night. And for God's sake, lay low. Fletcher's all over the place, and he's not exactly a team player. I don't always know where he's going to be from one day to the next."

I took the business card and stood to go.

"Are you all right?" he asked me suddenly. His eyes were brown and moist, the eyes of a protective German shepherd. "Do you need money or . . . anything?"

I felt the bristle of shame. "I'm fine. I can take care of myself. I just need to get Parker out of jail, that's all."

He didn't say anything as I rose from the bar stool.

I'd already started for the door when I turned back. "Why are you doing this?" I asked him. "Why are you helping me?"

He stared into my eyes for a long time before answering. "I have a daughter. She's a bit younger than you, but not so young that I can't see where a few bad choices could take her." He paused, seeming to choose his words carefully. "I don't like what they did to you. And to Parker."

It was the first time anyone other than Parker had thought us innocent. Or, if not innocent, at least less guilty than Cormac and Renee. It didn't change anything. Not really. But I felt a loosening of the guilt that had wound its way around my heart, trailing through the rest of my body like a parasitic vine, threatening to strangle me. I wanted to thank him for seeing something in me that I couldn't see in myself, but I couldn't speak around the lump in my throat. I felt his eyes on me as I disappeared into the crowd.

Ten

I took the long way back to Torrance, getting off at the Marriott a half mile away from my hotel and sitting in the coffee shop for an hour before getting on another bus. I didn't think anyone was following me, but I knew at least part of my confidence was based on Detective Castillo and the feeling that I could trust him. I wanted to believe it was true, but there was too much at stake to take anything for granted. Especially now.

I was beat by the time I finally walked into the lobby of the Motel 6. I paid for two more nights, trying not to panic as I pulled two hundred and forty more dollars from my bag. I'd planned to approach Selena by now, beg her for a place to hide out while I figured out my next move. Now the thought made me nervous for more than one reason: I still felt sick at the idea of having to face her after what I'd done, but I had to worry about Detective Fletcher, too. If he was digging into the case, Playa Hermosa was the last place I should stay. I decided to wait until my next call with Detective Castillo. If he managed to place Cormac in Seattle, going to Selena might not be necessary. I could broker a deal with the prosecutor and then Parker and I would be free. I headed for the elevators, promising myself that if Detective Castillo didn't find Cormac, I'd go to Selena for help. It would suck, but I wasn't exactly overflowing with other possibilities.

I spent the next two days making lists on my computer of every job Parker and I had done with Cormac and Renee, every detail, every stop we'd made. I played back conversations in my head, wishing Parker were there to contribute to the meager list of things I thought I'd heard, names I might or might not have remembered correctly, places Cormac and Renee had mentioned in passing while looking at each other in ways that in hindsight might have been meaningful.

I left only for food, bringing it back to my room, where the curtains were never open more than a crack, the bedside lamp on at all hours of the day and night, the TV muted. I worked for hours at a time, putting everything into a spreadsheet and using the VPN to google anything I wasn't sure about, hoping that something would ring a bell in my mind. When my eyes burned with exhaustion, I fell onto the rumpled bedsheets, my mind racing, the results of my online searching still seared behind my eyelids. Then I would turn up the TV and stare blankly at it until I fell into a sleep so profound, I woke up feeling drugged.

By Sunday morning, I had a short and meaningless list of words and names. None of it meant anything to me, and I tried to stifle the desperation that threatened to drown me on the way to the Galleria to call Detective Castillo. I probably could have called him from the hotel, but I was still being extra careful. If he hadn't found Cormac in Seattle, who's to say that he wouldn't experience a sudden reversal of his "I don't like what they did to you" routine?

I took the stairs to the top of the parking garage and dialed his cell phone number. He answered after the first ring.

"It's me," I said.

"Grace. How are you?"

"I'm . . . fine. What did you find out about Seattle?" Nice guy or not, I didn't want to stay on the phone any longer than I had to.

"It's not good news. The woman? Miranda Mayer? Said Cormac left last week. Said they went to the theater and his daughter was gone when they got home. The next day, he was gone too. My contact in Seattle asked around, but as of now, there's been no trace of him."

The hope that had been building inside me dissipated all at once, leaving me deflated and tired. I should have known. No way would Cormac stay put, a sitting duck, while someone who knew where he was went rogue.

"Any idea where he might have gone?" Detective Castillo asked.

"None." The time for mincing words was over.

I heard him sigh into the phone, could almost see him run a tired hand over his face the way he'd done a couple of times in P.F. Chang's. "Did you come up with anything on your end?"

I took out the folded piece of paper where I'd written my list. "Just a bunch of stuff that doesn't make sense."

"Like what?"

I hesitated. If I gave him what I had, ridiculous as it was, and any of it turned into a real lead, would Parker and I get credit for it? Would I still be able to use it to get him out of jail?

"I want to know what kind of deal I can get for Parker before I say anything else," I said.

"Grace . . . I can't promise you anything. Not without something solid. Do you have something solid?"

I looked down at the piece of paper.

Raymundo (Phoenix)
Geneva (Chicago—IDs?)
Morenovich (sp?)
Jeffries (money?)
Royal (DC/Baltimore)

The names and words had been said in passing between Cormac and Renee.

Did you call Raymundo?

Morenovich should have that data by tomorrow.

I have to drive out to Geneva tonight.

But I hadn't been paying attention at the time. I'd been too firmly ensconced in my belief that I was safe, that the carefully orchestrated details of our life were in such good hands that I didn't need to worry, let alone ask about any of it.

"I wouldn't say solid," I finally said in answer to Detective Castillo's question.

"Can you give me an idea what we're talking about here?" he asked.

"It's just . . . I don't know. Names and stuff," I said.

"First and last names?" he asked.

I was surprised by the bitter laughter that escaped my lips. It sounded strange and foreign. "I wish."

There was silence on the line between us. "Listen, Grace. I could tell you that I can get you a deal. And then I could take what you have and hope to get something out of it. If we do, it may or may not help Parker. But the truth is, you have a better shot if you come to the DA with something solid, especially with Fletcher on the case."

I chewed my lip. "What would you consider solid?"

"The names and addresses of the people helping Cormac and Renee, the people giving them information they need to pull jobs like the one at the Fairchild place. And if you can get a better line on Cormac's whereabouts—or Renee's—so much the better."

"Fat chance of that," I muttered into the phone. Cormac was a pro. When he wanted to stay gone, he stayed gone. And Renee might as well have been a ghost. I wouldn't even know where to start looking for her.

"There is one more option," he said.

"What is it?"

"You could turn yourself in. Throw yourself on the mercy of the prosecutor, back up Parker's allegation that the two of you were just kids following orders from the only parents you'd ever known."

"What would happen then?" I asked.

There was a beat of silence before he spoke again. "Hard to say. You might do a little time in a juvenile correctional facility—I think we could argue that would be best given your age—and Parker might get a little less time than he would otherwise get. But there are never any guarantees."

Parker and me in jail—Detective Castillo could call it a "juvenile correctional facility," but everyone knew that was just another word for jail—was not what I'd had in mind when I'd come back to LA. We'd have records for life, records that would make it hard to get jobs or credit, things we would need if we were going to live straight.

"I can't risk it," I finally said.

"Grace . . . I'm worried about you. A young girl on her own isn't a good thing in this world."

I looked at my phone. I'd been on the line for almost three minutes. "I've been alone a long time," I said, preparing to disconnect the call. "I just didn't know it."

Eleven

The next afternoon, I was back on the bus to Playa Hermosa. I'd spent the night before counting my money and rehashing the conversation with Detective Castillo, which led me to the same inevitable conclusion: I was at a dead end.

I had no idea how to use the little information I had to help Parker, but I couldn't keep blowing a hundred and twenty dollars a day on a hotel. I toyed briefly with the idea of taking to the streets, sleeping outside. It was warm enough. But then I realized how easy it would be for the cops to pick me up—or for something even worse to happen to me—while I was asleep on a park bench. The thought of approaching Selena, of facing her after what I'd done, made me feel like screaming inside, but I was out of options. As much as I hated to admit it, I needed help.

The sun had broken through the marine layer when I got

off at the Town Center and began walking up the winding hills toward Selena's house. The air was moister and heavier than usual, and I was grateful for the canopy of trees that offered me shade every few feet.

I had turned the corner onto Selena's street and was heading for my hiding place under the arbor when I spotted a peacock standing in the middle of the road. It was so still it could have been fake. A moment later, it blinked, its eyes never leaving my face.

I slowed down, totally exposed, the cover of the arbor forgotten as I stared at the bird. I'd forgotten how magnificent they were up close. Pictures never really did them justice. On paper they were just two-dimensional objects that hardly seemed real. But in real life their plumage was enormous, the green and blue tail feathers vibrant and iridescent, standing a good two feet above their regal heads or dragging four feet or more behind them. Their eyes were deep brown, wise and knowing, and they never seemed in a hurry to get anywhere, even when the cars on the peninsula honked and people screamed out their windows at them to move.

"Hello," I said softly. I couldn't shake the feeling that it was the same bird that had wandered Camino Jardin in front of the house we'd rented while working the Fairchild con. It didn't make sense—Camino Jardin was at least a mile farther up the peninsula—but I felt a strange kind of kinship with the animal, set loose in a foreign land and forced to make its way around people who didn't want it there, because it had nowhere else to go.

The sound of my voice seemed to waken it from its reverie, and it started to move, strolling calmly across the street and disappearing around the corner like it knew exactly where it was going.

I stared after it, feeling something tug at the hollow place in my chest. Then a car backed out of one of the driveways, and I hurried forward, head down, making my way to the arbor that had shielded me on my last failed trip to see Selena.

I glanced down at my phone, trying to look busy as the car continued down the road. When it was out of sight, I tucked myself back into the arbor and took stock of the situation on Selena's street.

The house I was standing in front of looked as empty as it had the first time I'd been there. The street was empty too, except for the same blue Range Rover. The sight of it there, in the same place it had been a few days earlier, rang the alarm on my instincts. It was just a car—and an empty one at that—but I'd been trained to notice things that were out of the ordinary.

I glanced up and down the street, looking for the car's owner, wondering why they hadn't parked in the driveway. Then again, maybe they were visiting someone. Maybe they were hired to clean house or dog sit while one of the home-owners on Selena's street was at work. It's not like someone was sitting inside the car with binoculars trained my way.

I was pulled from my paranoia by a flash of movement at the corner. At first I thought it was the peacock, but when

I turned toward it I realized it was Selena, alone again and heading for her house.

She was wearing capris and a drapey tank top, her hair pulled back into a thick curly ponytail. She didn't look like herself, something I hadn't been able to see when she'd been covered almost head to toe in her raincoat. When we'd run from Playa Hermosa just before Christmas, Selena had been curvy and lush, her skin as creamy as caramel. Now her arms seemed pale and thin, and her pants hung low and loose on jutting hip bones. More than that, her face wore an unfamiliar expression, her eyes blank, her mouth down-turned as she walked. Where was the Selena I'd known? The one with light in her eyes and an aura of expectation, like the next good thing was right around the corner, something she seemed to believe even when she'd seen bad things happen up close and personal?

I took a step forward as she turned onto the walkway leading to her house. I forced myself to put one foot in front of the other, to cross the street, to continue up the pathway behind her. I'd never really be ready, and while her dad was probably at work, I couldn't risk ringing the doorbell once she was inside. I had no idea what she would say or do if she saw me through the peephole on the big front door, if she would have time to get to the phone and call the cops.

She was digging around in her bag, probably looking for her key, when she froze. I was just a few feet behind her, my heart flapping like a wild bird. I almost wondered if she could hear it.

She slowly turned to face me, and all the words I'd planned flew from my mind. We looked at each other for a long minute before she spoke.

"You better come inside."

Twelve

I stepped into the foyer and looked around, wondering how a place that had once felt like home could feel so foreign, so changed. Then I realized it wasn't Selena's house that had changed; it was me. I wondered suddenly how all the things I'd done in my life would look if I were to revisit them, if all the choices that had seemed so clear to me then would look different through the lens of everything that had happened, everything I'd done.

"My dad's not here," Selena said, watching me look around the foyer. She dropped her book bag on a bench near the door. "Come on."

I looked nervously around as she started down the hall. It was hard to imagine Selena betraying me, telling me no one was home so her dad would see me and call the police, but I didn't deserve the old consideration of our friendship, and I knew it. I wouldn't blame her if she turned me in. Still, I had no choice but to follow her to the kitchen.

The room was neat and modest, a stark contrast to the gourmet kitchens, loaded with commercial-grade appliances and designer granite, that were standard for most of the houses in Playa Hermosa. I used to love sitting here with Selena, drinking iced tea and talking about life and school.

Selena gestured to the table and chairs in front of the big picture window. "Have a seat." She was being polite, but her eyes were empty, her voice flat. "Want some iced tea?"

"Sure."

She poured us each a glass and set mine down in front of me. Then she leaned against the counter and folded her arms over her chest. I knew body language—I'd studied it as part of our many cons—but Selena's would have been readable even by an amateur. It screamed defensiveness, a big flashing sign that read STAY AWAY.

Silence sat heavy between us. Finally I said the only thing I could say.

"I'm sorry to come here."

She studied me for a minute. "You've got balls. I'll give you that."

I shook my head. "It's not like that."

She shrugged. "What do you want me to say, Grace?"

I looked down at the table and blinked back the tears that sprang to my eyes. "Nothing. I just . . . well, first I want to say I'm sorry."

"That's it? You're sorry?"

"I don't know what else to say. What we did was fucked up, and I'm not making excuses, but—"

"But now you're going to make excuses," she said.

"It's . . . more complicated than it seems."

She took a drink of her tea and set the glass down a little too hard on the counter. "Did you or did you not lie to us—to *me*—about who you were, about why you were here?"

"I did," I said softly. It was true, but I still hated admitting it out loud.

"Did you use what you learned from hanging out with us to steal from Logan's family?"

I looked into her eye. "Not you, Selena. I never used anything you told me. You weren't even supposed to be part of the plan."

She narrowed her eyes at me. "What does that mean?"

"Just . . . I was assigned to get in with Logan and Rachel and the others, try to get information on Logan's family. But I . . . well, I liked you. And I wanted to be your friend even when it seemed like a bad idea."

"Well, I wish you'd listened to your gut, Grace. It would have been a lot easier for me."

The words stung because they were true. It was something I hadn't thought about at the time: that my friendship with Selena was completely self-serving. She'd never been part of the con. I'd pulled her into my web of lies because I'd needed her friendship, even when I knew it would be temporary. She hadn't gotten anything but trouble out of the deal.

"You're right," I said. "I'm sorry."

"Stop saying that," she snapped. "It doesn't change any-thing."

"I know."

"Why was it complicated?" she asked.

I looked up at her. "What?"

"You said it was complicated. Why?"

I shook my head. "You were right. It's not complicated. I did what I did. The why of it doesn't really matter."

"No, it doesn't," she said. "But I'd still like to know."

Somewhere outside the window I thought I heard the caw of a parrot, and I turned my face to the glass, searching the trees for the flash of blue or red that would signal its presence. Like the peacocks, the parrots had been let loose here a long time ago. Now they were naturalized, as at home on the peninsula as if they'd been here for centuries, another mysterious resident of a place that never seemed quite real.

"I didn't really know my mother," I finally said, still looking out the window. "I was in foster care for a long time. I moved around a lot, had a lot of different families. Some of them were nice. Most of them weren't."

A host of people flashed through my mind. Harsh faces and blank stares, cold hands and dirty sheets.

"I was eleven when Cormac and Renee adopted me," I continued. "They were heaven compared to the other people I'd been with. It was the first time I'd had a real family, one that couldn't be taken away from me."

"Did you know what they were going to do?" she asked.

"Not right away. And when it first started, it was small. Like a game."

"A game?"

I heard the bitterness in her voice and shook my head. "That's not what I mean. I'm not telling this right. They would teach me and Parker—"

"Parker was adopted by them at the same time?"

"No, he came later, and for a while it felt like we would be a normal family. Then they started teaching us little things. Sneaking into the movie theater, conning the bus driver into giving us a free ride, lifting wallets." I shrugged. "I was twelve. It seemed like a game, a challenge. By the time the jobs got bigger, it just kind of seemed like that *was* normal."

Her expression didn't change. "But you had to know it was wrong when you got to the big stuff. You're not a kid anymore."

I swallowed around the shame that clogged in my throat. "I know. And you're right: I did know—do know—that it was wrong. I just . . . I didn't know how to get out of it. They were the only family I had."

"Some family."

The comment hit me where it hurt. They weren't my family. Had never been my family. Except Parker. He probably would have bailed on Cormac and Renee long before the Fairchild con if he hadn't felt responsible for me.

"Parker was in the same boat. He was already thirteen when Cormac and Renee adopted him, and he had a history of suicide attempts in foster care." I hated telling Parker's secrets, knew he'd hate me for using them to gain Selena's sympathy. But I'd do anything to win his freedom, even if he wouldn't. "It's not right that he's in jail while Cormac and Renee are free."

"He committed a crime," Selena said. "Someone died."

"Parker didn't kill that guard. Even the police know that. And he wasn't at Logan's . . . at the Fairchild house the night of the theft."

She shook her head. "It doesn't matter. He was part of it. An accessory."

"So was I." I said it softly, afraid to remind her of the fact in case she decided to call the cops.

"I know. And I should turn you in right now."

"Why haven't you?" I asked her.

She looked away. "I don't know." We sat like that for what seemed like forever. Finally she turned to look at me. "What do you want, Grace?"

I bit my lip, tried to remember the words I'd rehearsed at the hotel. But they were gone, a yawning blankness in their place. "I'm trying to help him," I started. "Parker, that is. But I don't have very much money for a hotel, and I was hoping—"

"Wait a minute. . . . You want to *stay* here?" She said it like I'd asked her to help me rob a bank.

"I . . . Well, I was thinking maybe the pool house . . . just while I figure things out . . . how to make some things right. . . ." The idea suddenly seemed stupid and naive. What had I been thinking?

Her laughter was short and dry, caked with bitterness. "Grace, no. I couldn't help you, even if I wanted to." She met my eyes. "And I don't."

I didn't know what to do with this colder, harder version of Selena. But it had been my doing. It was only right that she would refuse to help me.

I stood. "I understand. And I don't blame you. I . . ." I looked down at the tile floor. "I'm sorry I asked, and I'm sorry for . . . for everything." I forced myself to look into her eyes. If I didn't look too hard, I could almost believe they were the same. Almost. "You were good to me. Better than I deserved. Whatever happens, I'll never forget that."

I made my way out of the kitchen and down the hall. I didn't know what I would do next, and the truth is, I didn't even care. Nothing hurt more than knowing I'd hurt Selena. And I had. I saw it in her eyes, however much she tried to cover it with anger. Even worse, I'd changed her, made her hard and cynical like me. Another thing I would never forgive myself for.

I opened the door and stepped out onto the pathway, hurrying for the sidewalk as I tried to hold back my tears. Coming here had been just another selfish thing in a long line of selfish things. I didn't need to add guilt to the mix. I was halfway to the corner when I heard her voice behind me.

"Grace, wait."

I turned to face her, surprised to see tears coursing down her face. "I thought you were my friend!" she shouted.

I swallowed hard. "I was. Just not the one you deserved."

"How could you?" she asked, a sob catching in her throat.

"How could you do that to Logan? To me?"

"I don't know." Looking at her face, at the pain in her eyes, was too hard. I looked down at my shoes instead. "I can't . . . I can't think straight right now. I'm alone and I'm desperate to help Parker. I'm just . . . taking it a day at a time."

It wasn't smart to stand outside, visible to anyone who might drive by or look out their window, but the weight of Selena's gaze pinned me in place, like a long-dead butterfly mounted for examination.

"Where are you staying?" she finally asked.

I wanted to tell her everything, but I knew it would be stupid. I heard Detective Castillo's voice: *He's been all over the case files, reinterviewing people, rescouting the scene of the crime.*

"I'm fine. I have a place for now."

She crossed her arms. "I can't believe you're putting me in this position."

"I know," I said. "I suck." I met her gaze and shrugged. "I just didn't have anywhere else to go. I'm sorry."

She bit her lip, fighting some kind of internal struggle in the moment before she spoke again. "If I let you stay, it's only to help the police get Cormac and Renee. I know you're worried about Parker, but Logan and his family deserve justice too."

I nodded, hardly daring to believe that she might help me. "I understand."

She sighed. "Okay. You can stay. But not for long."

Thirteen

I checked out of the hotel and returned to Selena's the next afternoon. I was nervous as I approached her house, half expecting the police to jump out of the bushes and arrest me on the spot. But the street looked like it had the last two times I'd been there, empty except for the blue SUV and a fuel-efficient hybrid that was totally out of the question as an undercover car for the police.

Selena opened the door before I had a chance to knock, like she'd been waiting for me. "Come on," she said. "You need to get settled before my dad comes home."

She led me down the hall, through the French doors off the kitchen and across the brick patio. The yard wasn't large, and the pool occupied most of the space between the house and the fence at the back of the property. The water looked cold under the shade of the cypress trees, and I had a flash of Selena, Harper, and Olivia floating in the pool on Camino Jardin while Rachel and I lounged on the patio.

We continued past the pool to a small bungalow sheltered by the trees at the rear of the property.

"The pool guys come every Wednesday," Selena said, "but the supplies are kept in the shed, so you should be okay as long as you stay hidden when they're here."

I set down my bag and looked around. It was one big room, with a small kitchenette on one wall and French doors that opened onto the pool area. The décor was what Renee would have called uninspired: an overstuffed sofa flanked by end tables, a coffee table, and an armoire against one wall. I liked it. It felt a little like my hotel room. Comfortable and featureless, with nothing to mark my identity, no reminders of the past, nothing to make me wish for a future I'd probably never have.

"What about your dad?" I asked.

"He never comes back here," Selena said. "It was built before we bought the house, but we don't really use it. Just be careful between seven and eight in the morning and six and seven at night. That's usually when he's going to work and coming home. And don't turn on the lights at night."

I nodded. "And the bathroom?"

She crossed the room and opened a door next to the kitchen. "It's small, but it'll do the job. Just don't turn on the water when my dad or the pool guys might hear it running." She walked to the kitchen and opened the small refrigerator that stood against the wall. "I put some food in here for you.

The sofa pulls out. There are blankets in the cabinet. Let me know if you need anything else."

She was trying to be conversational, but there was a cold undercurrent to her voice that made her sound almost like a stranger. I didn't expect anything more. I was lucky she'd let me stay at all, and I knew it.

"Thank you," I said. "Really. I don't know what I would do without your help."

Her throat rippled as she swallowed, and she looked at the floor. "Do you know how long you'll need to stay? I . . . I don't want to get my dad in trouble."

"I'll be as quick as I can. I just need time to track some of Cormac and Renee's sources. Detective Castillo—"

"Detective Castillo?"

"Do you know him?" I asked her.

"He interviewed us," she said. "My dad and me."

"Well, I called him," I explained. "To see if there was some way to trade information for Parker's release. But he said I didn't have enough. I need to have details: people Renee and Cormac used to help them set up their cons."

"And you don't have any of that?" Selena asked.

"It's stupid, but I never . . . well, I never asked. Actually, I never insisted. I *did* ask questions in the beginning"—I was just now remembering it—"but they made it clear that Parker and I were on a need-to-know basis."

"Yeah, *their* need," she said.

I nodded. "Exactly. So I have to try and remember some things, details about what they did and how they did it.

Otherwise Parker's going to go to jail for the crime all of us committed."

"What if you turned yourself in?" she asked.

"I've thought about it. But how would that help Parker? We'd both be in jail, and Cormac and Renee would be out there, lying and stealing, hurting other people." I shook my head. "I'll take my share of the blame when the time comes, but to help Parker, I need to get everything I can first."

She seemed to consider my words as she looked around the room. "I better get back to the house. Do you have a cell phone?"

"I bought a new one when I got here," I said. "A cheap one with no plan."

"I'll give you my number. If you need anything, you can text me. I can always make an excuse to come outside or sneak out after my dad's asleep."

We exchanged numbers and she headed for the door.

"Selena?"

She turned around. "Yeah?"

"I know don't have a right to ask, but how is Logan?" The words threatened to stick in my throat. "How is his family?"

A shadow seemed to pass over her face. "Logan's dad has been in Shady Acres since a few days after they found out what happened. His mom is . . . Well, you know Leslie; she's strong."

I nodded, ignoring the vise around my heart when I thought of the woman who'd been so nice to me while I was using her son. Shady Acres was just a pretty name for one of the only places that could deal with Warren's brand of paranoid psychosis. He had been there before, and I'd helped send him back. Now Leslie and Logan were alone.

"And Logan?" I braced myself for the answer. I wanted him to be okay, to have moved on. It would hurt, but he deserved that.

"He's not good, Grace." My face must have shown my dismay, because she kept going. "What did you expect? He's hurt about what you did to his family, to him, and he's mad at himself for being so stupid, for not seeing what none of us but Rachel saw. But I don't think any of that is what really kills him."

I wasn't sure I wanted to know the answer, but not asking the question would make me an even bigger coward than I already was. "What does?"

"He loved you, Grace," she said softly. "How is he supposed to live with that?"

Fourteen

I spent the first day at Selena's holed up in the bungalow, hyperaware of every noise outside. I was careful to be quiet, to only run the shower when I was sure Selena's dad was at work, but a constant cloud of anxiety still followed me as I slept, ate, and showered.

There was no TV in the armoire, but there were a few old books, and I chose an old copy of *The Awakening* to pass the time. Selena never made an appearance, and I wondered if that was how it would be for the duration of my stay: Selena keeping her distance while I lived in the bungalow, invisible to the outside world. It was what I'd wanted, but it still felt strange to be hidden away.

By the second day, I felt a little bit more relaxed. I texted Selena for the password to the house's Wi-Fi and opened my laptop. Then I opened up the file with my list of clues.

Raymundo (Phoenix)
Geneva (Chicago—IDs?)
Morenovich (sp?)
Jeffries (money?)
Royal (DC/Baltimore)

They didn't mean any more to me now than they had when I'd first made the list. Cormac had mentioned someone named Raymundo—or maybe Raymond?—when we were in Phoenix. I thought it had something to do with cars, but I couldn't remember if he'd been talking about a repair to the cars we were driving then or the purchase of new vehicles for the Fairchild con.

The other stuff was no better. A conversation between Cormac and Renee about visiting someone named Geneva when we were in Chicago. A sarcastic comment about consistently slow information coming from Morenovich. Cormac, complaining about intel in New York from a person or company that went by the name Jeffries (first or last name? The name of a company? I didn't know). And last, Renee running out late one night in Baltimore, telling Cormac she'd make the pickup at Royal.

None of it meant a thing to me.

Frustrated, I closed my laptop. I wanted to see the trees and hear the ocean crashing against the cliffs of the peninsula. To walk and walk as I worked through the names and places on my list. But there were only the four beige walls of the bungalow, the soft hum of the fridge, the distant whir of the pool's filter outside.

I looked at the time on my phone. 11:47. Selena wouldn't be home for a while, not that it mattered. I hadn't seen her since she'd brought me back to the bungalow. And her father wouldn't be home until much later. It was Wednesday, but the pool guys had already come and gone. It only took me a few seconds to come to a decision.

I washed my face and brushed my teeth, then stood over my backpack, surveying my outfit options. I only had three choices: the angsty grunge clothes I'd been wearing when I left Seattle, the capris and tank top from my Playa Hermosa wardrobe, or a skirt and T-shirt that would fit in anywhere. I chose the skirt and T-shirt combo, making a mental note to stop in at a thrift store to buy a few things. I'd been washing my clothes in the bathtub and hanging them to dry, but they were starting to look wrinkled and dingy, and I needed at least a couple more options if I didn't want people to think I was a homeless waif.

Once I was dressed, I stuffed my laptop and everything else into my backpack. It felt heavier after a few days of downtime, but I didn't dare leave anything behind. Detective Fletcher could be out there. I could be arrested on the street. Someone could find my stuff in the bungalow and call the police. Selena could have a change of heart and do it herself. Anything could happen. When it did, whatever it was, I wanted to have my stuff. It wasn't much, but it was mine.

I closed the door of the bungalow and edged my way

around the side of Selena's house, keeping an eye out for jogging moms, landscapers, detectives conducting interviews. An unfamiliar girl on the street was one thing. An unfamiliar girl leaving the fenced-in backyard of an affluent dentist in Playa Hermosa was another.

No one was there, and I continued down the street and headed for the Town Center. I picked up the bus and rode it all the way to Hermosa Beach, where I walked to a diner on the strand.

I was exhilarated to be outside, comfortable among the eclectic mix of surfers and hippies, Rastafarians and soccer moms. I chose a table outside, then ordered breakfast and a carafe of coffee. I had just opened my laptop, hoping the change of scenery would clarify one of the clues, when I saw the man on the strand.

Something—a loose string, a wrong note—twanged inside of me at the sight of him. He was slender and agile, walking toward the café with a casual but purposeful stride. He wore chinos and an obnoxiously loud Hawaiian shirt. His eyes were hidden behind aviators, his head covered with thinning strands of gray hair. He turned to look out over the water, and I had a flash of another man, face concealed beneath a straw hat, steam rising around him in the Jacuzzi.

It couldn't be.

He was about ten feet away when I realized he was whistling. I recognized the melody not as belonging to a certain song, but because it sounded eerily similar to the melodies whistled and sung by the man next door to us on Camino

Jardin. The tune was slow and a little sultry, a perfect match to the way he strolled down the strand.

I watched him from behind my sunglasses, my pulse racing as he came closer. He would pass me. He would walk right by without even looking my way. It was just a coincidence. I told myself all of these things even as he turned onto the patio of the café and walked directly toward my table.

The world seemed to tilt, a low humming building in my brain like it had when I'd almost passed out at the fast-food place in Lomita.

He slid into the chair across from me and took off his sunglasses. "Hello, Grace. Is it time to call in reinforcements?"

Fifteen

I didn't say anything for a full minute. I was trying to reconcile the fact that the man sitting across from me was the same man who had lived next door to us when we'd been planning the Fairchild con. The man who had sung strange songs and talked to the parrots like they could understand him, whose verbal meanderings had always seemed directed my way, even when I knew it was crazy to think so.

"What are you doing here?" I finally asked. Then I registered that he knew my name, and I put my hand on my laptop, ready to run. "Who are you?"

He put both hands on the table and leaned toward me, his blue eyes rheumy but sharp. "I understand why my appearance might come as a surprise, but I mean you no harm."

"You didn't answer my questions." I forced my voice steady and held his gaze. People took advantage when they thought you were weak, even if they didn't mean to. Unless the person in question was the kind who thrived on being needed. Then you could pretend weakness to get their help. But I already knew the man in front of me wasn't that kind of person.

He leaned back, studying me. "My name is Marcus. And from your reaction, I'd say you remember me."

I closed my laptop and put it in my bag. "I do. I just don't know why you're here. How did you find me? And how do you know my name?"

"I know a lot of things," Marcus said.

The words caused a flash of memory, and I suddenly heard Rachel Mercer's voice in my head, back in the days when we were circling each other, Rachel trying to put her finger on why she was so suspicious of me while I did everything I could to deflect her suspicions.

I know lots of things, Grace. Lots and lots of things.

"Like what?" I asked him.

He fiddled with the sunglasses in his hands, pursing his lips as he considered his words. "Let's just say your dear old dad and I go way back."

It took me a minute to figure out what he was saying. "You know Cormac?"

The sound of his laugh startled me. It was so genuine. Like he really thought it was funny. "I know him better than anyone. But his name isn't Cormac. I imagine you've already thought about that."

I hadn't, actually. In spite of all their lies, Cormac and

Renee were still Cormac and Renee in my mind. Stupid. But with the knowledge of my own naivety came something else, something unexpected: hope. Here was someone who knew Cormac. Someone who might have information that would help me find out more about him.

A waiter appeared at the edge of our table. He looked at Marcus. "Would you like a menu?"

Marcus shook his head. "Just coffee."

The waiter disappeared.

"What's Cormac's real name?" I asked, wondering if it might be a clue to his whereabouts.

The ghost of a smile touched Marcus's lips in the moment before it disappeared again. "You've been trained by the man you call Cormac. A man who, for all his other faults—and let's be honest, there are too many to name here—is a professional. That makes me think you must be a professional, too. And a professional knows that information is a commodity. Something to be used and traded. Not something to be given away."

I shrugged. "I don't have anything to trade."

He leaned in, lowering his voice to a purposeful whisper. "Now, Grace, I don't believe that."

The waiter reappeared with a cup of coffee and set it in front of Marcus. "Can I get you anything else?"

"No, thank you," Marcus said.

"What do you want?" I asked when he was out of earshot.

"Actually, I think our goals are somewhat . . . aligned at the moment," Marcus said. "Which is one of the reasons

I'm here: to make you a proposition."

"A proposition?"

He looked out over the water, his expression belying his boredom. "A scheme or plan of action, a joint project or task."

"I know what a proposition is," I snapped. "It was meant as a rhetorical question. A way to get you to say more."

He looked back at me, the boredom gone from his face, replaced by what I would have sworn was interest. His nod was a gesture of apology.

"Right. As I've said, we have the same goal. You want to find information about Cormac—"

"How do you know that?" I interrupted.

"That's not important," he said.

His words made my face flush hot with anger. I picked up my bag and stood. "I've spent the last six years doing what Cormac and Renee told me to do, letting them pat me on the head and tell me that not knowing anything was for my own good. It hasn't gotten me anywhere. If you want me to talk to you, you'll have to be straight with me. Starting now."

His unruly eyebrows rose in surprise. He met my eyes for a long moment before speaking. "After years of trying to track Cormac, I finally got a lead on his destination through a mutual . . . associate. From there it was a simple matter of looking at the rentals available on the peninsula."

"You knew we were coming to Playa Hermosa before we got there." I didn't know whether to be freaked out or impressed.

He nodded. "The house on Camino Jardin was bugged

before you ever arrived. As you now know, I was your neighbor. When you left, I lost track of you all for a while. Except for Parker, although I do have someone keeping an eye on him in jail." I barely had time to digest this new piece of information before he continued. "But I had a feeling you'd be back. You and Parker seemed too close for you to leave him behind, and you hadn't been with Cormac long enough to learn his brand of disloyalty."

I heard the note of bitterness, the only real emotion he'd shown during our conversation, in his last sentence.

I sat down. "What do you mean you have someone keeping an eye on Parker?"

He reached for his coffee cup but didn't pick it up. "My former profession means that I usually have acquaintances in jail. I have a friend in County who's been watching Parker for me." He finally took a drink of his coffee. "Tough kid."

I leaned forward. "Is he okay?"

Marcus shrugged. "As okay as can be expected. He hasn't pissed off anyone too important. Not yet, anyway. That's something."

I looked down at the table. I was relieved to have some kind of word about Parker, but I wasn't sure how I felt about someone watching him, and I definitely didn't like the idea of someone watching me.

"How did you know where to find me today?" I asked.

"I've had someone watching the Rodriguez and Fairchild houses. A few days ago, my contact informed me that you'd approached your friend—Selena, is it?" Now it was his turn to ask the rhetorical question. Marcus knew Selena's name and address, and probably a whole lot more about her and Logan. "Once I picked up your trail again, it wasn't difficult to follow you here."

I nodded. "Go back to the part about you and me having the same goals."

"It's simple," he said. "You want information on Cormac. So do I."

"Why?"

He turned the ceramic coffee cup in his hand. "He was nothing but a street hustler when I met him: stealing wallets, picking pockets, buying merchandise with stolen credit cards and returning his purchases for cash refunds. But he had potential. A lot of it. I saw that right away."

"Wait . . . you trained Cormac? Taught him?"

He looked up. "I was quite a bit younger then, and I admit that my initial interest in Cormac was . . . romantic."

My shock must have shown on my face, because he hurried to correct my mistaken understanding of the situation.

"Oh, no!" he laughed. "The attraction was purely one-sided, but who could blame me? He was a fine-looking man." He took a drink of coffee. "And it didn't matter that he didn't return my feelings. He was good. Very, very good. Before long he was moving onto bigger jobs, longer cons. We were a team. I'd never made as much money as I did with him."

"What happened?" I asked, because something obviously had happened.

"He met your mother." He glanced up, startled. "I'm sorry. I suppose you don't think of her that way anymore."

"I don't know how I think of her," I admitted. "It doesn't matter. Keep going."

"Well, he met your mother and fell in love, and soon the two of them were hatching their own little schemes." He shook his head. "Even on the grift, everything comes back to love. And sex."

I ignored his final words. The last thing I needed was to think about Cormac having sex. With Renee. With Marcus. With anybody. "So what? You stopped working together?"

"I'm afraid it wasn't as neat as that," Marcus said, taking a drink from his cup. "Cormac left. But not before he stole the take from the biggest job we'd worked together."

"He stole from you?"

Marcus nodded. "We were supposed to meet after the job, but when I got there, he was gone. And so was the money, although he did leave a charming note."

I thought of the hours after the Fairchild con. Cormac and me arriving at the motel that was supposed to be our meeting spot, only to find a single gold bar and a note from Renee that simply read, *I'm sorry.*

Talk about karma.

"Ah, I see I've struck a chord," Marcus said, watching my face. "Did Renee make a similar exit, then?"

I sat up straighter. I wasn't telling him anything until I knew what he wanted from me—and what I could get in return.

"I'm sorry for what Cormac did to you, but what does it have to do with me?"

"Very little. The past is the past, after all." He waved a hand dismissively in the air. "But it goes to our shared goal: you want information about Cormac and his sources, presumably to help Parker. I want the same thing."

"Why? To get your money back?"

He laughed. "We both know how Cormac spends money. Not to mention the woman who called herself your mother." He shook his head. "No, I'm sure the money from our joint venture is long gone."

"Then what?"

He met my eyes, and I had the feeling he was thinking, trying to decide how much to tell me. "It's like I said: our goals are aligned, if not exactly the same. You see, I don't just want information on Cormac." He hesitated. "I want to bury him."

Sixteen

I leaned back in my chair and turned my eyes to the beach. People rode by on bikes, glided past on Rollerblades. Little kids made their way to the sand with buckets and shovels in hand, hats on their heads to protect them from sunburn, and teenagers talked and flirted as they leaned against the concrete wall that lined the strand.

I didn't belong here. I would never be that carefree. Would never really be young again. My only chance was a fresh start somewhere, and I couldn't get that without my freedom. Mine and Parker's. I couldn't stay with Selena forever, and I couldn't get a job or even finish high school without a new fake ID, a purchase that was way out of reach with the little bit of money I had left, assuming I could even find someone to do it.

The only way to freedom was to out Cormac's sources in

exchange for amnesty, but thanks to my apathy in the years I'd been with him and Renee, I couldn't do it by myself. I didn't even have a starting a point. I needed help, and the pickings were pretty slim.

I looked back at Marcus. "How do I know you won't bail on me, too?"

Something seemed to soften in his eyes. "I suppose you don't," he said. "I can only tell you that I'm not Cormac. Our . . . philosophical differences were the thing that drove a wedge between us. Cormac has no boundaries, no rules. Nothing was ever off-limits." He rubbed the scruff at his chin. "I am considerably older than Cormac, and I like to think I've learned a few things that he hasn't. One of them is that you can only chip away at your own soul for so long before it crumbles. And once it's gone, it's gone forever." He shook his head. "There are some things I just won't do, but since I don't expect you to believe me, perhaps you can rely on good old common sense."

"What do you mean?" I asked.

"Cormac spent the last year of our alliance developing his own sources. That's part of why it took me so long to find him. You're one of the few connections I have to him now. Without you and the knowledge you possess—knowingly or otherwise—I'm at a dead end. And I don't like dead ends." He watched the people walking by on the strand. "Not enough escape routes."

It made sense, but I was still nervous about working with someone else. The last time I'd had partners, Parker had gone to jail and I'd ended up on the run. "Can I think about it?" I asked.

He hesitated before nodding. Then he pulled a pen from his pocket and started writing on one of the napkins. "Call within forty-eight hours if the answer is yes. Leave a message with a number where I can reach you, and we'll arrange a time to meet and get started." He folded the napkin and extended his hand. When I closed my fingers around it, he held on. "Can I trust you not to go to the police with my offer?"

I nodded. "I'm not looking to hurt anyone. The only reason I'm doing any of this is to get Parker out of jail. If I decide not to work with you, I just won't call, that's all."

He let go of the napkin, and I stuffed it in my bag.

He put his sunglasses back on and stood, digging in his pocket for a minute before throwing a twenty-dollar bill on the table.

"It's a beautiful day," he said, looking out over the beach. "You should try to enjoy it. Our vocation is difficult. Have to find pleasure in the little things." He turned his face toward me, but his eyes were lost behind his sunglasses. "You be careful now, Grace."

He turned and walked away, whistling as he merged with the crowd moving north on the strand. I watched his Hawaiian shirt bob through the masses until it finally disappeared in the sea of bathing suits and board shorts.

Seventeen

The conversation with Marcus replayed in my mind as I took the bus back to Selena's. I felt vindicated. My paranoia about the man next door on Camino Jardin hadn't been crazy after all. My instincts, honed by Cormac and Renee, had been right on. Now Marcus was my only link to a world I once thought I knew like the back of my hand. However much I hated the idea, I needed him. But if he was telling the truth, he needed me, too.

It was after three when I got off the bus at the Town Center. I was tired and overwhelmed, my mind spinning with everything Marcus had told me about Cormac and Renee. A year ago, I wouldn't have believed they could leave a partner high and dry. Now it didn't surprise me at all, and I wondered if Marcus had felt as surprised and betrayed as I did when Renee abandoned us. I was still thinking about it when I saw the man standing outside Mike's.

I knew right away that it was Detective Fletcher. He was big, bigger even than Detective Castillo. His arms, jacked in a snug T-shirt, were crossed over his chest, his legs slightly apart where he stood, like he was in ready stance for some kind of attack even though he was just standing there, talking to a guy in an apron who probably worked at Mike's. I could sense Fletcher's coiled energy even across the parking lot, could feel the intensity of his eyes even though they weren't directed at me.

For a minute, all I could do was stare, my flight response stalled by the panic flooding my body. The guy with the apron nodded, and Fletcher raised his head, slowly turning my way as he gazed absentmindedly over the parking lot. I put my head down and hurried for the crosswalk, trying to look purposeful instead of scared, just another kid coming home from school or the beach.

I had to fight the urge to run as I made my way up the peninsula. I felt Fletcher at my back, like he was stalking me from the Town Center, even though there was no sign of him the few times I dared to look back. By the time I sneaked back into the pool house, I felt dizzy, my head roaring with the blood in my veins.

I put my bag down on the floor and went to the fridge, where I removed a bottle of water. I downed the whole thing in one go and collapsed onto the sofa. I hadn't bothered opening it up to the bed. I was scared I'd have to make a quick exit, and I didn't want to get too comfortable. I curled onto my side and listened to the hum of the pool filter and the rustle of leaves in the trees that hung low over the pool house.

I must have dozed off, because the next thing I knew I was sitting up, alert to a noise I was sure I'd just heard. Was it Fletcher? Had he followed me to Selena's after all? I waited in silence, prepping myself to run. A moment later, it came again: a soft knocking from the door.

My heart beat like a drum as I picked up my bag and crossed the room. I stood to the side of the door, waiting. Then, three short knocks, followed by a forceful whisper.

"It's me. Selena."

The air seemed to leave my lungs all at once. I was about to open the door when I stopped, wondering if it could be a trick. Maybe Selena was surrounded by a SWAT team or something. Maybe they were just waiting for me to open the door to take me into custody. There was no peephole on the pool-house door. No way to be sure Selena was alone.

"Are you going to let me in?" she whispered again.

Then again, if the police were here, it meant the place was already surrounded. And if the place was surrounded, I was done. I could read people's body language, lift wallets, ingratiate myself with any high school crowd, but this was real life. I wasn't the star of some action movie who could escape the police by using my surroundings or throwing stuff in their way to slow them down.

"Hurry up!" she whispered. "My dad will be home soon."

I opened the door a little and peered through the crack.

Selena stood there, hair wild around her face.

I stood behind the door as I opened it wider, just in case anyone was watching from one of the surrounding houses. Selena stepped inside.

"What took you so long?" she asked when the door was closed.

I hesitated. How could I explain the fear that pervaded my every waking moment? The way my breath caught in my throat if someone looked at me a little too long, a little too hard? The knowledge that Fletcher was close, and that if he took me into custody, I wouldn't even have anyone to call for help and Parker would be as good as convicted?

"I saw a cop at the Town Center," I finally said. "It was some guy named Fletcher. Detective Castillo told me Fletcher has been assigned to work the Fairchild theft with him, and apparently, he's pretty enthusiastic about finding new leads."

She frowned. "Did he follow you?"

"No, it just . . . made me nervous." I hesitated. "I wasn't sure you were alone."

She studied my face. "If I wanted to turn you in, I would have done it already." She sat down on the sofa. "We should probably have a code, some way for me to signal you if there's trouble."

"You could text me."

"True," she said, "but I'm thinking about an emergency code. A way for you to know if someone's with me outside the pool house, just in case everything happens fast and I don't have time to text you."

"That makes sense," I agreed.

"How about three knocks if I'm alone, one knock if someone is with me?"

"One knock seems like a bad idea," I said. "I don't want to freak out if one of the pool guys brushes up against the building or something."

"True." She seemed to think about it. "How about four knocks if I'm alone, two if someone is with me?"

"That works," I said.

"And I'll never use your name," she added. "Just in case one of the neighbors is listening."

I smiled a little. "You're pretty good at this."

"Yeah?"

I nodded. "Not that I recommend it as a life path or anything."

She looked around the pool house. "It does seem to have limited career potential."

I couldn't help laughing, and for the first time, when she met my eyes, she was smiling a little, too. "I'm not letting you off the hook," she said softly, her expression pained.

I looked down at my hands. "I know that."

"You hurt people, Grace. You hurt me."

The now-familiar lump had again lodged itself in my throat. "I know. I don't even want to say I'm sorry again, because I know it doesn't cut it, and it just seems . . . insulting to keep saying it. Like it's enough when I know it isn't." I looked up and met her eyes. "You know?"

She nodded. "You said you wanted to help Parker. That that's why you're here?"

"Yeah."

"How will you do that?" she asked. "How will you help him?"

"I have to have something to trade. Something solid that will lead the police to the sources Cormac and Renee used to set up their jobs."

"But you already said that you don't have that stuff."

I bit my lip. "I don't. Not really."

"So what will you do?"

I thought about Marcus. "I don't know." I sat at the other end of the couch. "I made a list of things I remember— phrases, names, anything that might be a clue. But it's not much."

She nodded solemnly.

"Let's talk about something else," I said, anxious to change the subject. The furrow on the bridge of Selena's nose told me she was thinking about my problem, and that was the last thing I wanted. "What's going on here? How is everyone?"

She sighed. "Let's see . . . Olivia's secretly seeing her private volleyball coach, and—"

"Wait!" I stopped her. "Seriously? How old is he?"

"Only twenty-two, but it's still a big deal."

"No one knows?" I asked.

"Well, *we* know," Selena said. "But her parents definitely don't."

My heart stuttered a little. I could see them now, everyone included in that *we*: Olivia, Harper, Rachel, Liam, Raj, and David. And of course, Selena and Logan. Still, I was happy Selena had remained part of the group after I left. When I'd first come to Playa Hermosa, she'd been a bit of a loner, and while she had seemed content, I knew that you could never have too many friends in this world, something that seemed even more true when you didn't have any.

"What about the others?" I was hungry for information about them. I wanted to picture Olivia's contagious smile, the expression on Harper's face when she thought hard about something, Raj's mischievous grin.

"Harper's still . . . well, she's Harper," Selena said. "You know how she is. She tries to play along with everything, but I think she's really sad inside. I haven't really figured out why. Raj's parents are making him go back to India for the summer, and Liam is going to some surf camp in Puerto Rico."

"Are they all ready for college?" I asked. It was hard to imagine it: everyone going out into the world, making new friends, changing and evolving into the adults they would all become.

"Yep. Olivia got into Brown. Harper's going to USC."

"What about you? Looking at schools yet for next year?"

She nodded. "I'm thinking Berkeley. But I'm volunteering in Nicaragua this summer, so who knows? I guess anything can happen."

"Wow . . . that's awesome," I said. "You're finally going to travel like you always wanted."

"Yeah, I'm pretty excited."

"What about David?" I asked. "Are you still . . ."

She nodded, and a secretive smile appeared on her lips. "We are."

"How's that?"

She hesitated. "Pretty amazing."

"I'm so happy for you," I said. "Really."

"Thanks."

I hesitated. "How about Rachel?"

She seemed to think about it. "Not very different from when you left. Just a little more self-righteous."

"She has a right to be." I was surprised that I wasn't mad. Rachel's snooping wasn't what had done us in. We'd done that all by ourselves. She had just been looking out for Logan. I could never be angry at her for that. "She knew what I was before anyone."

Silence settled over the room as we avoided discussing the one person we were both thinking about.

"Will Logan be okay?" I finally asked. I wanted to be told that I hadn't ruined him and his family completely. That there was still hope for them to be like they used to be. I knew that probably wasn't the answer I would get, but I also knew that I couldn't hide from what I'd done.

Selena looked down at her hands, picked at the loose skin around her thumbnail. "I'm not sure we should talk about Logan. It will only make you feel worse."

"I want to know."

"He's . . . I don't know. He does all the same stuff. You know—he surfs with the guys and meets us at Mike's and comes to parties. But he bows out a lot, too. I think it's because of his mom. Because he's worried about her being alone."

"And?" I prompted, sensing there was more.

She sighed. "He's just sad. He tries to hide it, but I know it's true." My chest felt excavated, cleared out of everything that had made me whole.

"Will his dad be okay?" I asked.

She shrugged. "I don't know. Logan doesn't like to talk about it."

I wanted to ask about Parker, if Selena had heard anything about him. If she knew he was okay. But it didn't seem right to show my concern for Parker on the heels of talking about Logan. Was I allowed to care about them both?

She sat up straighter, the brightness in her eyes seeming a little forced. "Have you heard about the peacocks?"

"No, but I saw one the other day. Out on the street in front of your house."

She nodded. "There's going to be a vote on what to do about them. People are really fed up with the noise and stuff."

"What's going to happen to them?" I thought about their eyes, those brown eyes that seemed to hold so much knowledge, to know exactly how I felt. Both of us outsiders.

"It depends," she said. "They'll either get to stay, or they'll be moved to some kind of animal sanctuary up north. Everyone's really worked up about it. I went to a meeting with my dad and thought a brawl was going to break out. Who would have thought a bunch of birds would cause the devolution of movie executives and tech millionaires."

"Crazy," I agreed softly.

Selena stood. "I better get inside," she said. "My dad will be home soon."

"Thanks for coming out to check on me. It was . . ." I hesitated, not wanting to make it weird. "It was nice talking to you."

She headed for the door. "Let me know if you need anything."

There was so much I wanted to say, but nothing came. I was paralyzed by my own guilt, by the feeling that I didn't have a right to say anything. That I'd given up the right to even exist in the same space as Selena and the others, to breathe the same air.

So I didn't say anything. I just watched her go and wondered how many more times I'd have to say good-bye.

Eighteen

The next afternoon I walked cautiously to the Town Center and took the bus to Redondo Beach. I wasn't crazy about being so visible, but I couldn't stay locked up in the pool house if I wanted to help Parker. Besides, the odds of Detective Fletcher being at the Town Center on two consecutive days were slim, and I was craving the ocean. Like an addict who'd taken one hit, I was jonesing for my old life in Playa Hermosa, trying to connect with it in the only ways I could.

I'd known the moment I opened my eyes what I had to do, and I got off the bus and headed for the cluster of shops in an area called the Riviera Village. I was still being paranoid, and I made a mental note to ask Marcus about the cell phone and whether a pay-as-you-go could be traced. The thought caused me to relax, not because I trusted Marcus, but because I'd finally have someone to commiserate with, someone to ask all the little things I didn't know about being on the run.

The marine layer was back, a damp blanket overhead that turned everything a muddy shade of gray. I ducked into a secondhand store, where I overpaid for two pairs of capris, three T-shirts, and a sundress. I would have preferred a Goodwill or Salvation Army—that was where the really cheap stuff was—but hell would freeze over before the locals would agree to have a real thrift store in their midst.

I left the store with my purchases and walked west, sitting on one of the benches that overlooked the beach. In front of me, a long retaining wall stood above the water with a steep set of stairs every hundred feet or so that led to the strand. The waves were calm, and I watched a few surfers catch the gentle swells, riding them a few feet before sinking slowly into the water.

Finally I took out my phone and dialed the number Marcus had given me, before I could change my mind. Someone picked up on the second ring.

"Yeah." The voice was male and gruff.

"Hello, I'm calling for Marcus."

"Number?" The guy sounded bored, like I was calling for a taxi or something. Remembering Marcus's instructions, I recited my cell phone number. The man hung up without saying good-bye.

I looked down at the phone and waited. It rang less than a minute later.

"Hello."

"How are you on this fine day, my dear?" Marcus asked the question like he cared about the answer, like he wanted to know that I was enjoying the weather.

"I'm fine," I said. "I'm calling to say yes. I'll work with you."

"Wonderful," he said. "Let's meet to discuss the details, shall we?"

"Sure. Where?"

"Where are you? I'll come to you."

I tried to think of a way to explain my location without being too obvious, just in case I was wrong about the phone. "A little north of where we were yesterday."

"Ah," he said. "I understand. Are you near the road?"

I glanced behind me, like I needed to make sure the street was still there even though I could hear the cars whizzing by at my back. "Yes."

"I'll be there in fifteen minutes."

He disconnected the call before I could say anything else.

I watched the seagulls fly circles over the water, turning and dipping, sometimes dropping to pluck something off the surface. I should have been nervous. I'd just agreed to work with Marcus, a man I didn't know at all. His desire for revenge and my desperation to save Parker were the only things that united us. Not exactly the makings of a solid business partnership.

But I couldn't muster the energy to care. Being afraid was exhausting, and I'd been afraid more often than not the past few months—probably the past few years, if I was honest. Now a kind of peace settled over me. I needed help, and I'd called the only person who was offering it. If he turned out to be a traitor or a liar, well, how much worse could things get?

About ten minutes after I'd hung up with Marcus, the sound of traffic behind me changed, the whoosh of cars driving by fading against the soft purr of an idling engine.

I turned to see a familiar blue Range Rover next to the curb. A moment later, the passenger-side window retracted with a hum, and Marcus's face appeared from the across the front seat.

"Get in," he said. "We'll go somewhere more private."

I picked up my stuff and walked slowly to the car. This was it. Moment of truth. For all I knew, Marcus would drive me right to the police station or hack me to bits and dump me in the nearest ditch. Not that it mattered.

I got in the car and shut the door, and Marcus merged into the traffic along PCH.

"I'm glad you called," he said.

I didn't know what to say. *I didn't have a choice*? *You are my last resort*? Neither seemed like a good way to start our partnership.

"I just want to get Parker out of jail," I said. "The sooner the better."

He nodded. "I understand."

"Where are we going?" I asked as he turned toward Playa Hermosa.

He glanced over at me, his blue eyes clear and alert. His

crazy hair was hidden under a bucket hat, the kind old men wore fishing in movies, and he had on another obnoxious Hawaiian shirt. "I'm taking you home. My home," he clarified. "I have a feeling you haven't had a decent meal in a while, and I've found that being hungry affects decision-making capability. Can't have a hungry partner now, can I?"

"I guess not," I said weakly. I couldn't tell if he was just nice or if it was some kind of act, like a creeper trying to get a kid in a van by offering him a lollipop.

We wound our way up the peninsula, passing Camino Jardin. I looked back as we passed the road we'd both lived on in the fall. "I thought you said we were going to your house."

"We are. My new house. I couldn't risk staying on Camino Jardin. Not if I hoped to find you and enlist your help. The house Cormac rented while you were here is still vacant, and the police were still doing drive-bys after you left." He turned onto a street called Colina Verde. "I wanted to be close in case you reappeared, but if you did, I didn't want to draw unnecessary attention, which is why I rented another place on the peninsula."

I turned in my seat to watch a peacock strutting calmly down the side of the street.

"Beautiful, aren't they?" he asked.

I nodded.

He pulled the Range Rover into a driveway behind a nondescript sedan. "Here we are." He turned to look at me. "You did a good job with your hair and makeup. We wouldn't have recognized you if we hadn't been looking, and I don't think anyone else will either."

I didn't have time to ponder his use of the word *we* as I got out of the car and followed him to the front door of a bungalow-style house. It was small but cute, with wood siding and large windows. The front yard was boxed in with towering trees and large bushes covered with tiny blue flowers. A winding stone pathway led to a carved wood door that was at least seven feet tall.

Marcus inserted a key into the lock and turned the knob, then held the door open so I could enter the foyer first. "Honey, I'm home," he called out. His voice held a note of silliness that seemed strangely in character.

The interior was cool and dim, the trees and bushes outside blocking most of the murky daylight. I looked past the two-story foyer, the curved wrought-iron staircase leading to the second floor, wondering who else was in the house.

"Be right there!" a muffled voice called from somewhere beyond the hallway.

Marcus turned to me and winked.

A moment later footsteps sounded from the back of the house. I peered through the shadows at the approaching figure until a man appeared, holding a dish towel. He was younger than Marcus, tall and broad-shouldered, with skin the color of roasted coffee beans. He smiled, flashing teeth so white he could have been in a toothpaste commercial.

He leaned in to kiss Marcus on the cheek. "Did you get the lemons?"

Marcus handed him a bag that I hadn't noticed before. "You say 'jump,' I say 'how high,' remember?" He didn't seem unhappy about the arrangement.

The man favored Marcus with a smile before turning to me. "You must be Grace." He held out his hand. "I'm Scotty. Come on back to the kitchen. You're probably starving."

Nineteen

Scotty bustled around the kitchen, finishing a salad while Marcus took steaks and corn on the cob to the grill on the back deck. I was tongue-tied by the strange situation, although I don't know what was weirder, the fact that I was in an unfamiliar house witnessing the kind of domestic intimacy I'd only ever seen at the Fairchilds' or the fact that we were all con artists. Or Marcus and I were, anyway.

"So every day he drove twenty miles over the speed limit on that road," Scotty was saying, "and three days in a row I gave him a ticket. Finally I said, 'Either you're going to ask me to dinner or I'm going to have your license revoked.' And the rest, as they say, is history."

"You're a police officer?" I said, my heart tapping out a frenzied rhythm in my chest. What was I doing here? I didn't know these people. What had I been thinking?

"Was," he corrected. "And don't let that scare you. I know all about Marcus's previous . . . endeavors. We went clean together."

"So Marcus isn't grifting anymore?" I asked.

"That was our deal: I quit the force, Marcus quit the business, and we started over." Scotty set tongs in the salad and tipped his head at the French doors leading to the deck. "Let's eat. Those steaks smell done, and if we don't stop him, Marcus will grill them until they're like charcoal."

I followed him outside. The backyard was green and lush. Flower beds curved along each side, a riot of red, purple, white, and orange. Jasmine bloomed close to the ground, releasing its scent across the lawn, and bird-of-paradise, an odd-looking flower with pointed petals that resembled a beak, jutted up from behind peonies and roses. A Buddha statue, serene in the lotus position, was visible behind some of the bushes. Bird feeders swung from the trees at regular intervals. I could picture Marcus filling them as he talked to the parrots.

"Did Scotty tell you?" Marcus said, turning away from the steaks still on the grill. "I traded a life of glamour and excitement to play house with a cop."

Scotty removed the tongs from Marcus's hands and pulled the steaks off the grill. "Don't act like you don't love it."

We sat around the outdoor table, and Scotty loaded my plate up with a giant steak and two ears of corn. My mouth watered as the steak's aroma rose from the plate, and I tried to restrain myself from cutting giant bites and shoving them into my mouth faster than I could chew. I was hungrier than I thought.

While we ate, we talked about Playa Hermosa, about the peacock controversy, and about Southern California beaches. I knew they were steering clear of Cormac and Renee, of the Fairchild con, trying to give me time to relax and eat, and for just a little bit I felt normal. Like I could be anyone, just an average girl having dinner with family friends.

Scotty was pouring more wine when Marcus finally spoke. "I've been looking into Parker's situation, and I'm guessing we have about six weeks before he goes to trial."

The words washed away my contentment as quickly as a rogue wave. Six weeks. That was all the time we had to figure out Cormac's sources, to come up with something to trade for Parker's freedom.

I set my fork down on my plate. "That's not very long." I looked around the backyard, nervous about talking outside.

Marcus glanced from me to the radio playing softly on the deck. "As long as we don't talk too loudly, the music will block our conversation outside, and we have a signal jammer in the house that prevents listening devices from picking up anything. But you don't have to worry here. I'm squeaky clean. Have been for years."

I nodded, still nervous after years of training by Cormac, who insisted we not talk outside of a designated War Room.

"I don't have enough information to lead us to Cormac's sources before Parker goes to trial," I said.

Marcus tapped his cigar onto the deck, and Scotty glared at him in disapproval. "We're not going after Cormac's sources."

"But . . . I thought that's what we agreed. To pool our information and go after Cormac's support network. Shut them down and trade the information for Parker."

Marcus took a long draw on the cigar, his face thoughtful, before answering. "The thing is, most of the people who support us are decent. They live by an honor code, only do business when it serves a certain purpose. It wouldn't be right to rat them out."

I shook my head, confused. "Then what am I doing here?" I had to force my voice steady, work to keep it from turning shrill. "I only agreed to work with you because I thought we wanted the same thing."

"We do," Marcus said. "You want Parker's freedom, right?"

I nodded.

"Well, I want to out Cormac." I was just beginning to get his point when he spoke again. "Which is why we're not going after Cormac's sources—we're going after him. And maybe Renee, too, although word on the street is she might be tougher to find."

I imagined Renee, reclining on a beach somewhere while the money from Warren's gold racked up interest in an offshore account. I wondered if she ever thought of me, if she ever felt bad about leaving me behind or if I had been just another mark. I hated myself for even caring.

"I don't know where Renee is," I said. "And I don't know where Cormac is, either. Not for sure. I mean, he was in Seattle the last time I saw him. But Detective Castillo said—"

Scotty lifted his eyebrows. "Raul Castillo?"

I nodded.

Marcus set his cigar in the ashtray on the table and leaned forward. "Do you mean to tell me you talked to the police?"

I swallowed hard, suddenly scared that Marcus might change his mind about working with me. "Only to Detective Castillo. And it was off the record."

"Off the record?" Marcus sighed. "Tell me everything."

I explained my phone calls to Raul Castillo and our meeting at the promenade, including the part about Detective Fletcher and my sighting of him at the Town Center. They didn't speak, didn't even interrupt me to ask questions. When I was done, Scotty stood to take our empty plates into the kitchen.

"How do you know Castillo didn't have you followed?" Marcus asked. "That he didn't tail you to the beach? Follow us here?"

I couldn't help but be insulted. "I'm smarter than that. No one followed me. Castillo didn't even follow me after our meeting. He left first, and I didn't go straight back to my hotel. And Fletcher definitely didn't follow me to Selena's house, or I wouldn't be here right now."

Marcus studied me without speaking.

"Look," I said, uncomfortable with Marcus's silence even though I'd been trained to sit through them, waiting for a mark to spill their guts, "I had to talk to somebody. I didn't know you then. I was alone. I needed information about Parker, about what I could do to help him. And Detective Castillo seems like he cares, like he wants to help me." I shook my head, feeling naive. "That's probably hard to believe."

Marcus shook his head. "Not hard at all, in fact." He sighed. "Okay, let's establish some ground rules before we get started."

The thought of rules made me angry. I'd lived by Cormac and Renee's rules, and look where it had gotten me. I needed Marcus, but that didn't mean I had to play the part of loyal puppy dog.

"I'm listening," I said.

"We'll keep it simple," he said as Scotty returned for the serving platters. "You don't contact Detective Castillo, or anyone from law enforcement, without speaking to me first and considering my suggestions for security protocol."

"Considering them?"

He nodded. "I'm a practical man. And you're a smart girl. I'm confident you'll do the right thing when our freedom is at stake. But the choice will be yours."

"Go ahead," I prompted.

"I'd like to suggest you move from Ms. Rodriguez's house. It makes you, and by extension us, vulnerable."

"I don't have anywhere else to go," I said.

"You can stay here—for now," Scotty said, setting a fruit tart on the table. "We have two guest bedrooms."

I looked down at the table. I knew it was risky to stay at Selena's. The pool people might hear me in the pool house. Her father could discover me. Selena might change her mind about helping me. And those were just the possibilities I could think of. But I'd started to hope that Selena and I might be friends again, that her visit to the pool house was the beginning of something new, a fresh start. What would happen to that if I left now?

"I'm not ready to leave Selena's," I said. "And I just met you." I cast a glance at Scotty, not sure why I felt the need to apologize to him for the slight. "Sorry."

"No apology necessary. I get it," he said.

Marcus drummed his fingers on the table. "All right. You'll stay at Selena's for the time being. But you give me your word that you won't speak of Scotty and me. Our security is intertwined now, yours and mine. I won't speak of you to anyone. Won't let anyone know you're back in town. But I need your word that you'll show us the same courtesy."

"You have it," I said.

"And if you get even a hint of trouble, you'll call us and come stay here," Marcus added.

"Okay. What else?"

"We share everything," Marcus said. "Every bit of information on Cormac and Renee and their operation. Nothing is held back. If we're going to be partners, we have to trust each other completely. I think I've demonstrated that trust to you. I'm counting on you to do the same."

"I will," I said. "I promise."

"Then I'd say we have a deal—if my terms meet with your approval, of course."

There was nothing snide in his voice, no hint of sarcasm.

I nodded, and Marcus raised his glass. "I propose a toast: to Parker's freedom," he said. "And to giving karma the little push it sometimes needs."

Twenty

Marcus insisted I go home and get a good night's sleep before we got started. I was relieved to see Selena's driveway empty, her dad not yet home from work, and I hurried back to the pool house, where I tried to read before falling into a deep sleep. When I woke up, I felt different, alert and even a little optimistic. I wasn't alone anymore. Now I had people and resources on my side. Freeing Parker felt more possible than ever.

It was just after nine in the morning when I knocked on Scotty and Marcus's door. They had offered to give me a ride, but I didn't want the blue Range Rover anywhere near Selena's street if I could avoid it. Marcus was right: my fate was intertwined with his. But I was connected to Selena, too, and I wanted to keep her as far away from what I was doing as possible. I fought against the voice in my head that said

I should take Marcus and Scotty up on their offer and stay with them. That I was putting Selena in danger by staying with her, especially with Fletcher combing the peninsula for clues. Deep down I knew it was true, but I was too happy to be near her again, to know the possibility existed for a conversation, even if it was just for a few minutes in the pool house before her father got home. I swore to myself that I would move if there was even a hint of danger.

"Good morning," Scotty said, opening the door. I stepped into the foyer and he led me back to the kitchen. "Have you eaten breakfast?" he asked.

"I had a granola bar," I said.

"That's not breakfast," he admonished. "Sit. I'll make you something while we wait for Marcus to come down."

I sat on one of the bar stools at the kitchen island and watched as Scotty went to work, taking out a frying pan and pulling stuff from the fridge. The morning sun was diffused by the trees outside the windows, and the kitchen smelled of coffee and toast. An old-fashioned radio played softly from the counter. I thought it might be tuned to a station that played the old music Marcus liked, but instead I recognized the sound of the National's "Fake Empire."

"I suppose it's little morose for first thing in the morning," Scotty said, following my eyes to the radio. "Do you like them?"

"The National? I love them," I said. "I just . . ."

He stopped moving, wielding the frying pan like a lethal weapon. "What?" He smiled, and I realized how small he seemed. Not in a bad way. It's just that his big frame and broad shoulders were somehow diminished by his smile, by the kindness that radiated from him like warmth from a bonfire. "You thought I'd like Marcus's music?"

I nodded. "It's the thing I remember most about him from Camino Jardin. He was always humming, singing."

Scotty nodded and put the frying pan on the commercial cooktop. "I have to admit that when I pictured the man of my dreams, he didn't look like Marcus."

I couldn't help smiling.

"What are you trying to say?" a lazy voice said from the doorway. "I'm not your knight in shining armor?"

Scotty laughed. "More like a thief in a bucket hat."

Marcus shuffled across the floor in a T-shirt and slippers, his skinny legs emerging from a pair of shorts. He sat down next to me. "Morning, kid."

"Good morning."

"Get some sleep over there in the pool house?"

"Yep."

"Good. We have a lot of work to do today."

Scotty set a cup of coffee down in front of him and lifted an egg out of the carton. He looked at me. "You do like eggs?"

I nodded, and he cracked the two eggs into a bowl and whisked them with a fork while a pat of butter melted in the frying pan.

"So what do you like to do, Grace? When you're not . . . working, I mean?" Scotty asked.

It was an easy question, but when I reached into my

mind to retrieve the answer, I was met with emptiness. It had been too long since I'd had the luxury of doing something I enjoyed. In fact, everything I'd done since being adopted by Cormac and Renee had been the product of a con. I'd taken piano lessons from one of our marks in New York, had tried photography to get close to a girl in Chicago. I'd even joined the lacrosse team—and gotten clobbered—just to get to know a target in Phoenix. Had I enjoyed any of it? I didn't know. Enjoyment wasn't part of the grift. I looked up, surprised to see Scotty still watching my face, waiting for an answer.

"I like to read." It was the one thing that was mine, that had carried me through five cities, more foster families than I could count, so many last names I could hardly remember them all. I might not have a home, might not recognize myself in the mirror, but I could always find a library, the bookshelf at the Salvation Army, and later, when I was with Cormac and Renee, a bookstore. Books never lied to me, never betrayed me, never left me alone and wondering what was wrong with me.

Scotty stirred the eggs in the pan with the spatula. "I like to read, too. We have a pretty good selection if you ever want to borrow something."

I smiled. "Thanks."

Scotty scooped the eggs onto a plate with buttered toast and a handful of strawberries. He pushed the plate toward me. "Want some juice?"

"Can I have coffee?" I asked. There was a mini coffeemaker in the pool house at Selena's, but I was afraid to use it. The smell of brewing coffee was a distinctive one, especially to people who loved the stuff. I didn't want anyone to follow their nose to the pool house.

Scotty nodded and poured me a cup of coffee from the machine on the counter. He set the cup in front of me and I took a greedy sip before tackling my food.

"So what are we doing today?" I asked.

"We're going to brainstorm," Marcus said. "Go over everything you remember, from before the Fairchild con and after it."

I looked around the room, scanning for open windows, for anything that might give us away.

"Grace,"—Scotty's voice was gentle—"you're safe here. Marcus has never been picked up."

"Never?" I asked.

"Listen, kid." Marcus's voice was wry. "I know I look older than dirt, and it's true I was in the business a long time. But I was careful. Real careful. As far as I know, none of my marks ever realized I was the one who stole from them, which, incidentally, is how it's supposed to be. I'm perfectly legitimate, have been for years now."

"So you don't use . . ." I was afraid to finish the statement, still spooked about talking so freely.

"A fake?" he asked, referring to the fake IDs that had allowed Cormac, Renee, Parker, and me to move so quickly from town to town, setting up new names along the way in case anyone caught on.

I nodded.

"Don't need it," he said. "When I say I'm clean, I mean I'm clean. Never did anything high stakes. Kept it small. Just enough to live comfortably and stash a little for the future."

I looked around the room. "So how do you, I don't know, *live*?" I felt rude asking, but I had a right to know what he was into if we were going to be business partners.

"We have legitimate investments," Scotty said. "So I guess you could say we're both retired."

It threw me a little, the normalcy of their lives. I'd always imagined my postgrift life as on the run, in hiding, and looking over my shoulder. That there might be something else was a possibility I almost didn't dare entertain. And anyway, I couldn't think about any kind of life right now. Not until I freed Parker.

"Why do you need to know about stuff from before the Fairchild job if we're looking for Cormac now?" I asked Marcus.

"You might remember something that will tell me about Cormac's patterns," he said. "Everyone on the grift has their favorites—people they prefer to use for IDs, logistical support, transportation. But there are different levels of support. At the top are the professionals. People who really know what they're doing. Then there are the people who are a little less experienced, a little less scrupulous, people you want to keep your eye on."

"Why would you use someone like that?"

"The sources at the top are expensive. Their level of

expertise offers an extra layer of security, but not everyone can afford it. If you can't, you have to use who you can afford. And the less experienced aren't the worst of them. There are other people—gangbangers who sell IDs on the side, criminals fresh out of prison who run chop shops to provide cars to people on the run. Those are people you really don't want to get involved with."

"But people do?" I asked.

He nodded, finishing his coffee. "People do. And we need to figure out who Cormac's been using—both before and after the Fairchild job. Then you'll have to tell me everything you remember about Seattle. Where you stayed when you first got there, who Cormac talked to, even what stores you visited." He slid off the stool. "You can think about it while I get dressed. Then we'll get to work."

Twenty-One

We set up in the living room. Marcus sat on one of the overstuffed chairs, his computer on the coffee table in front of him, while I sat on the couch with my laptop. I wondered about the cushion that sat on the floor against one wall. The tiny Buddha statue and incense burner next to it made me think it might be for meditation. I assumed it was for Scotty. It was hard to imagine Marcus meditating.

We started at the beginning—the very beginning—with my adoption by Cormac and Renee. Marcus wanted to know everything: How many visits did they have with me before agreeing to the adoption? Where did they take me immediately after the adoption was final? How long did we stay there? How long before Parker was adopted? Where did we eat when we went out during that time? Where did we stay? What kind of car did we drive? How long after Parker was

PROMISES I MADE

adopted before Cormac and Renee started teaching us to grift?

Most of it seemed unimportant. I couldn't see how the restaurants we'd eaten in or the car we'd driven six years ago mattered now. But I answered anyway, pillaging my mind for information that had been dead to me, details about things I hadn't bothered to think about when they were happening, let alone in the years since.

I was already exhausted when Scotty brought in a tray of sandwiches, fruit, and two big glasses of water. He set everything down on the coffee table and reached for the TV remote.

"Water?" Marcus said, staring balefully at his glass. "Where's my Scotch?"

"You know what the doctor said." Scotty didn't even look at him as he turned on the TV. "Besides, I've been following the news in the other room. I think there's something you might want to see. "

I reached for my sandwich, surprised I could be hungry after the breakfast Scotty had served me just three hours before. I froze, my hand halfway to the plate, when the local news sprang to life. Parker was there, walking into the courtroom in an orange jumpsuit, his chin jutting defiantly. His forearms were bare, the leather bracelets he'd worn to cover the scars from his repeated attempts at suicide gone. That hurt me the most. Even more than seeing him in prison garb, seeing him handcuffed and escorted into the courtroom by a bailiff. Parker didn't like other people to see his scars. He

141

didn't want anyone to know that life had come so close to beating him. That he wasn't very different from the rest of us.

It was old footage, and a voice sounded over the image of Parker making his way to one of the tables at the front of the courtroom.

"The trial of Parker Dawson, alleged con artist in the December 2014 theft of twenty million dollars' worth of gold from Fairchild Industries heir, Warren Fairchild, will begin June twenty-ninth in Los Angeles Superior Court. William Bradley, a security guard for Allied Security, was killed during the theft. Dawson claims no knowledge of Bradley's murder. The district attorney's office for Los Angeles County has released a statement saying that an investigation is still under way and more charges may be forthcoming."

The image on the screen changed to one of a beached whale in Redondo, and Scotty turned off the TV.

Parker Dawson. So now they knew Parker's real name. All his secrets were laid bare for everyone to see, and I suddenly felt sick, the sandwich forgotten. "June twenty-ninth . . . that's only five weeks from now," I said softly.

Scotty sat down next to me and put a gentle hand on my back. "I'm sorry, Grace. We'll figure something out." He looked at Marcus. "Won't we?"

Marcus nodded. "We'll sure as hell try."

"Why don't you take a break?" Scotty suggested. "Have some lunch."

I shook my head and picked up my computer. Parker wasn't sitting in a cushy house in Playa Hermosa, eating a gourmet sandwich and drinking water. He was in jail.

Sleeping on a hard bed and eating crappy food. Deprived even of the privacy he needed to feel safe and protected. "We can work while we eat," I said.

Marcus hesitated, then took a bite of his sandwich and leaned toward his computer.

We moved into the years following Parker's adoption, working our way through the details of every con, beginning with Lansing, Michigan, the location of our first job. Marcus asked questions, making notes as I talked. If I forgot a detail or couldn't be sure about something, I'd look it up on my computer before passing the information to Marcus. We'd worked our way to Baltimore when Marcus asked, "Are you sure?" for what felt like the thousandth time.

"Yes, I'm sure!" I practically shouted. "I'm as sure as I can be, okay?" The extraction of details from my murky past was a painful exercise. My head hurt, and my body was stiff from sitting all day. More than that, my heart felt raw and wounded. Not because of what Cormac and Renee had done to Parker and me, but because I'd been forced to face every lie I'd told on the grift, every time I'd used or hurt someone. I thought I'd remembered them all, that I'd owned up to all the things I'd done. Turns out I was wrong.

Marcus raised his bushy eyebrows.

I sighed. "I'm sorry. I'm just tired."

He closed his computer. "Let's call it a day. Scotty has dinner going. You can eat and head home, get some rest for tomorrow."

We ate on the deck, listening to music and the sound of the birds calling to one another in the trees. We didn't talk much, but I didn't mind. It was an oddly comfortable silence given the fact that we hardly knew each other. Then again, maybe everyone else was just as tired as me.

Marcus insisted on driving me home, and I sat in the front seat of the Range Rover, clutching the container of leftovers Scotty had insisted on packing for me. I asked Marcus to drop me off one street over from Selena's house, and he pulled over to the curb and put the car in park.

"You never told me his name," I said.

Marcus looked over at me. "Whose name?"

"Cormac's," I said. The question had been bothering me ever since I'd heard the newscaster say Parker's name. "The first day we talked on the beach, you said Cormac wasn't his real name, but you wouldn't tell me what it is."

"It's Peter," Marcus said.

"And Renee?"

He laughed a little. "Hell if I know, kid. She's been Renee as long as I've known her."

I looked out the window, trying to attach the name Peter to Cormac's face. I couldn't do it. "Will the name help us find him?" I asked.

"Probably not. I doubt he's ever gone back to it."

I sighed. "Well, I guess I better go," I said, reaching for the door. "See you tomorrow."

It was nearly seven, and I kept my head down as I walked, knowing the evening commute was in full swing and hoping Selena's dad wasn't already home from work. I had turned the corner onto Selena's street when I saw the poster stapled to the light pole.

PROTECT YOUR QUALITY OF LIFE!! it screamed. I stepped closer to the poster and stopped walking, my concern about being seen temporarily forgotten.

Underneath the headline was a picture of a peacock, but it didn't look like the birds I'd seen on the peninsula with their soft brown eyes, their calm, meandering strut. The one on the poster looked bigger and more ominous, its eyes small and mean. My gaze moved to the text underneath the picture.

After years of complaints, the town of Playa Hermosa is finally hearing arguments regarding the possible relocation of the peninsula's wild peacocks. While these animals may seem tame, they are a frequent cause of car accidents due to their tendency to stand in the middle of the road. Furthermore, their squawking threatens to drive down property values in the area. THIS IS YOUR CHANCE TO BE HEARD by town officials. A meeting will be held on June 25th at seven p.m. in the town clerk's office. Please attend to PROTECT YOUR WAY OF LIFE on the peninsula.

My gaze returned to the peacock. The claims made in the poster weren't lies exactly. But the peacocks were just doing what they had to, trying to survive in a habitat that had probably been paved and developed right before their eyes. They'd been here for decades. It was home to them now. Wouldn't moving them, forcing them to adapt to another environment, be cruel? And for what? So the residents of Playa Hermosa didn't have to slow down, to take care as they drove around a bird in the road? So they didn't have to hear something other than the sound of their own voices?

But that wasn't fair either. Not everyone on the peninsula was arrogant or selfish. There were people like Selena, like Logan and his family, like Marcus and Scotty. It was hard to imagine any of them being on the side of the meeting organizers who wanted to banish the peacocks.

A sleek blue Mercedes glided past me, pulling into a driveway down the street. The sight of it pulled my thoughts away from the poster, and I continued to Selena's house, stepping onto the shady path and hurrying to the backyard. I was almost to the door of the pool house when I heard a voice behind me.

"I was getting worried."

I turned to see Selena standing with a plastic grocery bag in her hands.

"You were?" I felt a little ping of gratitude.

She nodded. "My dad went to the farmers' market yesterday. I thought you could use some fruits and vegetables."

I took the bag. "Oh, wow . . . thanks. That's awesome."

Her eyes dropped to the plastic container in my hands. "What's that?"

I looked down at the leftovers Scotty had packed for me. "Just . . . some leftover food."

A smile touched her lips, but there was suspicion in her eyes. "That doesn't look like restaurant takeout."

I wanted to lie. It would be easier than the truth, which was basically that I couldn't tell her anything. I wouldn't compromise Marcus and Scotty by telling anyone about them, wouldn't even say I had help in case I was caught and the police found out. Then they might search the peninsula, start looking too closely at its residents. Marcus and Scotty didn't deserve that. But I wouldn't lie to Selena again either.

"It's not," I said. "I went to dinner at a friend's."

"A friend's?"

I nodded, oddly insulted at the tone in her voice, like it was impossible to believe I could still have friends. It was irrational. She had every right to assume I was alone in the world. Until a couple of days ago, I had been.

"You haven't told anyone you're staying here, have you?"

I heard the fear in her voice and a wave of regret washed over me. "I told two people." I hurried to continue as disbelief hit Selena's face. "But they're completely trustworthy! I promise."

"You promise?" she snapped. "You promise. And I'm just supposed to take your word for it?" Her voice had gotten too loud, and she looked around the backyard before returning her gaze to me and lowering her voice. "That doesn't exactly inspire confidence, Grace," she hissed.

I swallowed hard. Sometimes telling the truth sucked. "I know. But it's true. I would never do anything to hurt you again. My . . . friends have more to lose than you do. They can't afford to say anything about where I'm staying."

She crossed her arms over her chest. "And you think you have the right to make that call?"

I sighed, exhaustion hitting me all at once. "No. I just . . ."

"What?"

I shook my head. "I wish things were different, that's all. I'm trying to do the right thing for once. Trying to protect you and make things right, and I'm just so . . . fucking worried about Parker. . . ." My voice broke a little with the weight of it. "I can't see him or talk to him. I can't make sure he's okay in there. I can't even tell him I'm here, trying to get him out." My shoulders sagged. "I'm doing what I can, Selena. If you want me to leave, I'll understand."

She looked down at her feet. "I'm sorry. I'm just scared."

"You have nothing to be sorry for. I couldn't ask for anything more than you're doing. I'm sorry that I scared you. Would you feel better if I left?"

She seemed to think about it. "Yes and no."

I laughed a little. "What does that mean?"

She took a deep breath. "I shouldn't care. I know I shouldn't. But I do. I care what happens to you, Grace. At least if you're here, I know you're okay. And you never know; I might be able to help."

I smiled. "You're already helping."

"What if I could do more?"

I shook my head sadly. "You can't. There's nothing anyone can do."

"I could visit Parker."

My heart seemed to stutter. "What?"

"I could visit him in jail. I wouldn't tell anyone here— like my dad or Logan or anyone—and no one else would think twice about it. We were friendly when he went to school here."

I banished the spark of hope that rose inside me. "I can't ask you to do that."

"You're not asking," she said. "I'm offering."

"But . . . why? After everything I did, why would you do any more to help me? To help us?"

Her throat rippled as she swallowed. "I don't know. I can't help caring about you, Grace. You were the best friend I ever had. And the truth is, it kind of seems like you got a raw deal." She looked up and met my eyes. "Not that I'm making excuses for you."

"No," I said. "I can't even make them for myself."

"But you and Parker . . ." She shook her head. "It's fucked up what Cormac and Renee did to you, what they made you do." I flinched a little at the sound of her cursing. In all the time I'd known her, I couldn't remember ever hearing her swear. "You were just kids. They took advantage of you. Used you."

Shame heated my cheeks. I'd always hated it when Parker claimed our parents used us. I felt accused, guilty. Like someone couldn't use me if I didn't let them, if I wasn't so weak that I made it possible. Sometimes I didn't know what was worse, being bad or being weak. Being *used*.

"Well, like you said, that's no excuse."

"I know, but that doesn't mean you don't deserve a little help." She looked into my eyes. "Let me do this, Grace."

Twenty-Two

I waited for Selena's father to leave for work the next morning before taking the bus into Torrance. Selena had told me that her dad kept Saturday hours for his patients, and I made a mental note to be back before four, when she said he usually came home. I needed some things from the drugstore, and I wanted to check in with Detective Castillo before I went to Scotty and Marcus's house.

I got off near the Econo Lodge and walked to Starbucks, where I sat down on the curb at the back of the parking lot and dialed Detective Castillo's number. He picked it up on the second ring.

"Detective Castillo."

"It's Grace."

There was a surprised pause on the other end of the phone. "Grace . . . how are you? Is everything okay?"

"Everything's fine," I said. "I'm working on . . . the stuff we talked about. On getting you the information."

"That's good, but listen"—he lowered his voice—"Parker's trial date has been set for June twenty-ninth. That doesn't give us much time, and Fletcher talked to someone on the peninsula yesterday who thinks they might have seen you."

All the blood seemed to rush to my head, Detective Castillo's words buzzing like a swarm of angry bees. "But I've been so careful . . . and how did they recognize me with the darker hair and stuff?"

"We don't know for sure that it was even you, but you need to be extra vigilant from now on. Legitimate lead or not, Fletcher's all over it." He hesitated. "Are you sure you don't want to come in? Take your chances with the DA's office?"

I thought about it. If it were just me, maybe. But I couldn't make that call for Parker. And now that I was working with Marcus, I felt more optimistic about our chances of getting Parker out of jail. It was a gamble, but it was one I had to take. More than that, I knew it was one Parker would want me to take.

"No, I'm going to get you what you want. Actually, I'm going to get you more than what you asked for. I'm going to get you Cormac."

"Grace, don't—"

"I'll call you back in a couple of days."

I disconnected the call and headed to Rite Aid. I filled my basket with toiletries and snacks, then caught the bus to the Town Center. When the bus dropped me off, I took a winding, circuitous route to Colina Verde, being careful to stay off the main arteries and busier roads. The sun was already hot and insistent, and by the time I got to Marcus's house, I was out of breath, my ponytail stuck to the nape of my neck with sweat.

"Grace!" Scotty said when he opened the door. "Are you okay? Get in here."

I stepped through the door. "Can I have some water, please?"

Lines formed on his forehead as he studied me. "You don't have to ask for something like that here, Grace. Come on."

He led me to the kitchen and filled a glass with cold water from the fridge. I downed it in one shot and finished another one before I finally started to breathe easy.

"What's going on?" Scotty asked. "Where have you been?"

"I had to go to town," I said. "I needed some things from the store, and I needed to call Detective Castillo so he didn't get worried and start looking for me. I just didn't realize how far away your street is from the Town Center."

"I thought you weren't going to contact Detective Castillo without talking to me first." Marcus's voice came from the doorway. He didn't sound mad, just walked to the counter and poured himself a cup of coffee before leaning over the island. He yawned, and it was obvious he'd just woken up.

"Oh . . . right." I'd forgotten all about that rule. "I'm sorry. I was in town and I wanted to get it out of the way. I'm never sure if my phone can be traced."

"Everything can be traced," Marcus said. "You can thank modern wiretap laws for that."

I felt my blood run cold.

"He's not telling you the rest." Scotty shot an admonishing look at Marcus. "They can tell which cell tower you've accessed, but that doesn't necessarily tell them where you are, especially if you make a point to move right after you make the call."

"Please tell me you made an effort to move right after you made the call," Marcus said drily.

I kept expecting him to yell or scream, to read me the riot act about protocol. I wasn't used to his blasé delivery, the feeling that he wasn't too invested in the outcome of anything. "I moved after I made the call," I said. "I chose a busy place in town, kept the call to two minutes, and then left right after I hung up."

"Good girl," Scotty said. "They can triangulate your call using the ping if they really want to, but it would take a little time, and they'd have to be really invested to get it done."

"How much time?" I asked.

Scotty thought about it. "At least fifteen minutes."

"I've always been gone by then," I said. "And anyway, I don't think Detective Castillo is looking to out me. Wouldn't he have to initiate the trace?"

Marcus nodded. "Since you called him directly, yes. But never count on the kindness of strangers."

"Isn't that what you are?" I asked, holding his gaze.

His face was impassive in the moment before a smile touched the corners of his mouth. "You're one smart cookie, you know that?" He slid off the bar stool and headed for the hall. "Back to work in T minus fifteen minutes."

I hesitated. "Marcus?"

He turned around. "Yeah?"

"Somebody on the peninsula told Fletcher they'd seen me recently."

Marcus raised an eyebrow. "Castillo tell you that?"

"Yeah."

He rubbed the stubble at his chin. "They don't have anything. It could have been anyone. But you should still make yourself scarce."

I nodded. I couldn't tell him I was already so scarce, I wondered if I even existed sometimes.

"Don't worry, kid," he said. "It'll be okay."

I tried to smile. "Thanks."

"He likes you," Scotty said when Marcus had disappeared beyond the doorway.

I laughed. "I don't know about that."

Scotty cast me a knowing smile and went to work on breakfast. He was sliding pancakes onto plates when he spoke again. "You know, I can drive you into town if you ever need something," he said.

I shrugged. "It's fine. I can take the bus."

He pushed one of the plates toward me along with a glass container of syrup. "You're very independent. Very self-sufficient. But everyone needs a little help now and then. And I'll tell you a secret."

I looked at him. "What is it?"

"I like helping people," he said in a conspiratorial whisper. I laughed, and he continued. "It's not like that old fool makes it easy to help him. I'm serious. I can give you a ride into town, pick stuff up at the store if you need it. All you have to do is ask."

I took a bite of pancakes. He made it sound so easy. You asked for help, and someone gave it to you. But that wasn't the way the world worked, was it? Cormac and Renee had made it clear that we had to stick together, that we could only count on each other. Listening to Scotty, I suddenly wondered if it had been another lie. Another way to keep Parker and me under their thumb, to make sure we needed them.

I finished my breakfast and met Marcus in the living room. We started where we'd left off, with the job in Baltimore, and continued all the way through the Fairchild con. When we got to what happened afterward, to Renee's betrayal and my flight to Seattle with Cormac, Marcus leaned forward. His questions got more intense, more pointed, his fingers tapping furiously on his keyboard as he made note of everything I said. When I was done, he sat back and shook his head.

"I know. It was a mess," I said. "Everything that could go wrong did."

"That wasn't just bad luck," he said. "Cormac was sloppy. He should have known better."

"What do you mean?" I asked. "What did he do wrong?"

"What didn't he do wrong?" Marcus laughed, but there

wasn't any humor in it. "Let's set aside the fact that he used two kids to help him." I winced. "He went into the Fairchild house not even knowing for sure that the gold was in the carriage house."

"But it was," I said.

"He didn't know that, and that's Grifting 101. You don't put yourself at risk—and you don't put the people you care about at risk—for a take you don't know is there." He sighed. "And the vandalism at Allied? Sloppy. He played Russian roulette with Parker's freedom, and Parker lost, not to mention the guard Cormac killed."

I had to swallow the acid that rose in my throat. I knew Cormac had killed that guard, but I'd never said it out loud. Never heard someone else say it out loud.

Marcus went on. "That's Cormac: never patient, always greedy."

I thought of Cormac's rush to get the gold, the insistence by him and Renee that it had to be that weekend, even though Logan wasn't leaving town with his parents. Even though it meant I had to drug Logan to give us enough time to get in and out undetected.

"Anyway, that will work in our favor now," Marcus said.

"How?"

"If he was sloppy on the job when he had resources available, he'll be even more sloppy now that he's on the run with hardly any money. He won't starve—Cormac will always be able to feed himself—but he won't have the luxury of hiding in an ivory tower either."

It was an entirely new take on Cormac. He'd seemed invincible when we'd been together, like he knew exactly what he was doing.

"What do we do now?" I asked.

"I'm going to put feelers out with some people I know, see if Cormac has reared his head in any of the usual spots."

"What can I do?"

"Nothing yet," Marcus said. "I need to process this information before I know which direction to run. You should rest, keep thinking about anything from Seattle that might help us. And think about Renee, too. My hunch is that she's long gone, but you never know. She may not have been able to get out. The police lowered the boom pretty fast."

For the first time, I considered the possibility that Renee hadn't been able to leave the country like we'd planned. I don't know why the idea bothered me so much.

Twenty-Three

I stayed for a late lunch, grateful Scotty gave me an excuse by insisting that he wasn't sending me home without a full stomach. I was already getting used to the comfort of them. To the cushy sofas and framed photographs, the Buddha statues that were secreted in little nooks throughout the house, the hint of incense hanging underneath whatever Scotty was cooking in the kitchen.

And I was getting used to Scotty and Marcus, too. Scotty always had a smile and had taken to touching me gently on the arm and calling me "honey" when I was upset or nervous. He was practical and efficient, the perfect foil for Marcus, whose gruff demeanor was laced with a kind of calm, a kind of acceptance, that seemed to transfer to me when we were together.

By the time Marcus drove me home, it was after three

and rain was falling from the sky in sheets, bouncing against the pavement and pummeling a drumbeat against the Range Rover's roof. He pulled over to the side of the road and reached into the backseat.

"Here," he said, handing me an umbrella. "You can bring it back tomorrow."

"Tomorrow? I thought we were done for a few days."

He looked lazily my way. "Listen, kid, my feelings won't be hurt if you have somewhere more exciting to be, but if you'd like a little company and a couple good meals, we're happy to have you."

I smiled a little. "Thanks. Maybe I'll stop by, then."

He nodded. "I'll contact you if I come up with anything on Cormac in the meantime."

I put my hand on the door and turned back to him. "Thanks, Marcus. For everything."

I opened the door and extended the umbrella before stepping out into the rain. Thunder rumbled in the distance, water streaming like a river down the gutters. My shoes and socks were soaked before I even crossed the street, and I hurried across the pavement, smiling to myself when I saw Marcus's SUV still idling at the curb as I turned the corner.

It was almost three thirty when I reached Selena's yard, and I was relieved to see that the Cadillac driven by her father wasn't in the driveway. Seduced by the comfort of Scotty and Marcus's house, I was pushing my return to the pool house every day. It was a dangerous game, and I silently chided myself for the recklessness, promising myself that I would be more careful.

I made my way down the path leading to the yard, retracting the umbrella as I stepped under the semi-shelter of the trees. I opened the door to the pool house and had just stepped inside when I heard the voice behind me.

"It's you."

I froze, the blood racing through my veins, my mind denying the voice even as my heart knew exactly who it was. I turned around slowly.

"Logan." The sight of him took my breath away. He stood a few feet from the door, the rain plastering his hair to his head. His cheeks were hollowed out, even gaunt, and there were shadows under his eyes. "What are you doing here?"

"What are *you* doing here, Grace?" He shouted it, and I knew instinctively that it wasn't just to be heard over the rain. That the sight of me had conjured up some kind of rage, had unmoored him in some way. I listened with horror as a sob stuck in his throat. "Why did you come back?"

I could only shake my head, not sure where to begin. Not sure how to begin. I stepped back, opening the door a little wider. "Come in, Logan. You're getting soaked."

He stared at me for a minute before swiping at his cheeks—was it tears or rain that streamed down his face?—and stepping through the door.

I closed it and turned to look at him. He was breathing hard, like talking to me, seeing me, required physical effort. I drank him in: the mossy-brown eyes that had once held a warmth meant only for me, the lips that had touched mine so gently. It was true that he had changed, that his face looked harder, his eyes shaded with pain that shook me to my core. But he was still Logan, and at that moment I didn't even care about the police, about the fact that Logan knew where I was, that someone else might know, too.

"Why did you do it?"

I'd done so many things, so very many things, that I wasn't sure what he meant. Why did I steal from his father? Why did I betray him? Lie to him? Drug him?

"It's . . . complicated." I hated myself for saying it. It was so trite, and I hurried to say something better, something that would explain the position I'd been in. "I told you the truth about Cormac and Renee. They adopted me, but there was more. They wanted Parker and me to help them . . . to help them steal from people."

He shook his head. "Did they threaten you, Grace? Did they force you to hook up with me? To act like you cared?"

"I did care; I—"

"Did they force you?" he shouted. But I knew that he already had the answer. Knew it from the way he looked at me. Like he didn't know me at all. Like he never had.

I swallowed the emotion that was lodged in my throat and shook my head. "No."

"Then don't ask me to feel sorry for you."

"I would never ask that, Logan."

"You . . ." His eyes bore into mine. "Do you know what you did to my father? To my family? Do you know what you did to *me*, Grace?" I nodded, but I knew it wasn't true. Not really. "Is that even your name?"

"It is," I said. "The Grace part, anyway."

His shoulders sagged, an expression of defeat passing over his features. "What are you doing here?"

My mouth had gone dry, and I had to dig for the words to answer his question. "I'm trying to make it right. To give the police information that will help them get Cormac and Renee."

He narrowed his eyes. "You're working with the police?"

"Not . . . not exactly," I said. He sighed and started to shake his head, like it was just another lie. I didn't want to get Detective Castillo in trouble, but I couldn't stand for Logan to look at me that way either. "I'm going to find Cormac, track him down, and give the information to the police."

"I thought you were with them," he said. "With Cormac and Renee. Or whatever their names are."

"I was with Cormac for a while. I don't know where Renee is. I don't know where either of them is now, not for sure. But I'm going to find out, about Cormac at least." Water was dripping from his hair onto his jacket, and I walked over to the armoire and pulled out a clean towel. I extended a hand to give it to him, and he stared at it for a few seconds before taking it. "Then I'm going to tell the police."

He laughed, bitter and sharp-edged. It didn't sound like him at all. "Now I get it. You want to help Parker. You're going to trade Cormac for him."

My face was hot with shame. "He's just like me, Logan. We were both adopted by Cormac and Renee, both . . .

pressured into doing what we did. He doesn't deserve to take the fall for all of us." I hesitated. Seeing Logan threw me, and I struggled to find the right words. "But I want to make it right, too. I want Cormac and Renee to pay for what they—for what *we*—did to your family. I'm willing to pay, too. As soon as I have the information I need, I'm going to turn myself in."

His eyes bored into mine, seeing all of me, just like always. Except this time, I didn't have any secrets. For better or worse, I was laid bare.

"And I'm just supposed to believe you?" he said.

I looked down at my feet. "It's the truth. I'm going to make it right. I might even be able to get your dad's money back."

He took a step toward me, and when I looked up, his eyes were brimming with so much loss, so much disappointment, that I felt it like a knife to the heart.

"Is that what you think this is about? Money? You don't get it, do you? We don't care about the money. You took something from my dad, from my family. Do you really think giving his money back will make it all right? That he'll be better, just like that?" He was crying now, and I felt tears slip from my own eyes. "It's not that simple, Grace. He's sick. And that's not totally your fault. He's been sick for a long time. But he was feeling good. He was feeling *safe*. That's what you stole from him. From all of us."

"I'm sorry, Logan. I'm so, so sorry. If you just . . . give me a little time here, time to find Cormac and bring him to the police, then he'll pay for what happened, and I'll turn myself in, I promise."

"I'm sorry, Grace. I can't. I just can't." He threw the towel on the floor and walked out.

I don't know how long I stood there, staring through the open door at the rain falling from the sky, before I grabbed my backpack and ran.

Twenty-Four

"Grace! What happened . . . ?" Scotty stared at me from inside the house.

I opened my mouth as a sob broke free from my throat, but I couldn't seem to get the words out.

"You're soaking wet!" He pulled me into the house and shut the door. Then his arm, strong and solid, was around my shoulders as he led me into the living room. "Stay right here. I'm going to get you a towel."

I looked down at the water streaming from my clothes and hair onto the expensive rug. "I'm . . . I'm wet. I'll get everything wet."

He put his hands on my shoulders and pressed me gently onto the sofa. Then he bent in front of me and looked into my eyes. "I don't care about that. Just stay here."

I sat on the couch and waited. My teeth clacked together,

although I couldn't say whether it was from the rain or some kind of shock. Logan's face was imprinted on my mind, tears mingling with the rain on his cheeks, the look of complete and total loss in his eyes.

"Here, honey." Scotty handed me a fluffy white towel and sat next to me on the couch. "Dry off. I have some tea steeping for you in the kitchen."

"Th-thank you," I said, still shivering. I blotted my hair with the towel and then draped it over my shoulders. "I'm sorry about the sofa. And the carpet."

He shook his head, but when I searched his eyes for annoyance, I saw only concern. "Can you tell me what happened?"

I started to try, and then it hit me: Logan knew I was in Playa Hermosa, knew I had been staying in Selena's pool house. I was compromised, which meant Scotty and Marcus were compromised, and Selena, too.

I bent forward at the waist, a low moan escaping my lips. "Oh no . . . Oh God . . ."

Scotty grabbed my arm, his grip firm but gentle. "You're scaring me, Grace. What's going on?"

"We have to get out of here," I gasped, barely able to speak the words around my fear. "Logan knows. He knows I'm here. He found me at the pool house."

Scotty looked into my eyes. "Tell me everything."

I skipped over the parts that caused me the most shame— the parts about ruining Logan's family, about being a liar and making excuses for myself. Scotty probably knew that stuff anyway, but I couldn't bear to say any of it out loud. I took deep breaths as I went, trying to keep myself calm.

When I was done, Scotty patted my knee and told me he'd be right back. He returned with a steaming cup of tea. "Drink this," he said. "It'll warm you up."

I looked at him. "Didn't you hear what I said? We have to get out of here."

"Did you tell Selena—or anyone else—about Marcus and me?" Scotty asked. He wasn't angry like I expected. In fact, he was perfectly calm, his voice low and gentle.

"No, but we can't take the chance," I said, my voice bordering on hysterical. "I couldn't . . . I couldn't stand it if something happened to you and Marcus because of me."

He put an arm around my shoulder and gave me a little squeeze. "Nothing's going to happen to Marcus and me. It's a free country. Even if Logan turns you in, they're not going door to door to see if anyone's hiding you. And Marcus and I have covered ourselves. We're just private citizens—a retired cop and his partner living off an old inheritance and its interest."

"What do you mean 'if'?" I asked. "Logan basically said that he was going to the police."

"People say things when they're hurt. He might change his mind." He hesitated. "How did he find you? Did Selena give you up?"

"I don't think so," I said. "Selena wouldn't do that to me. I just . . . I know she wouldn't. And Logan seemed almost surprised. Like he hadn't really expected to find me there."

"Then how did he find you?" Scotty asked. "If there's a breach somewhere, we need to find it and plug it."

"I have no idea," I said. "But I can't go back to Selena's."

He patted my shoulder and stood. "You'll stay with us. You'll feel better after some dry clothes and a nice, long rest. Everything always looks better after a good sleep."

I looked up at him. "What about Marcus?" A coil of fear unwound in my stomach. If Marcus was anything like Cormac, there would be hell to pay for the breach, even if it hadn't been my fault. And it had, because if I hadn't insisted on staying at Selena's, Logan probably wouldn't have found me. "He's going to be so pissed."

"Let me handle Marcus," Scotty said. "He's out right now, but everything will be fine, I promise."

I wanted to believe him, but I knew it wasn't that easy. Things weren't always okay just because someone said they would be. Sometimes everything unraveled despite everyone's best efforts. Despite my own. Then again, sometimes you didn't have a choice except to believe. Sometimes *not* believing would open up a well of despair so deep and so dark that you might never find your way back from it.

"Come on," Scotty said, holding out a hand.

Twenty-Five

The light was gray when I woke up in the guest room. I lay in bed for a few minutes, my eyes traveling the walls, a pale green almost the exact same shade as the foamy water that rushed around my feet at the Cove.

The room was large and comfortable, outfitted with a writing desk near the window, a large armoire, and a dresser with a mirror. There was a watercolor on the wall: a half-open lotus flower, its petals silken violet. All of it looked old and well-worn. It gave me a strange kind of comfort, imagining someone else opening the dresser drawers, sitting down at the desk to write a letter, waking up to the lotus.

A wind chime rang soft and low from the backyard, and the drapes billowed on either side of the slightly open window. The breeze passed over my face like a gentle hand. Next to the dresser was a door that I knew led to a private

bathroom. I had changed into dry clothes there before texting Selena and dropping onto the pillowy queen-size mattress. I'd fallen asleep almost instantly.

I reached for my cell phone, surprised to see that I had
four texts from Selena.

I'm so sorry. I didn't know he was coming.

**He found a search on my computer for LA County Jail. I
was looking up how to visit Parker. Please tell me you're ok.**

I'm worried.

Text me back!

It was 8:32 a.m. I'd slept through the night, and I suddenly had a vague recollection of darkness, the wind blowing forcefully through the curtains, muffled voices down
the hall.

I'm ok, I texted Selena. **But Logan's going to turn me in.**

I got up and went to the bathroom, then walked to the
door and opened it a crack. I stood there, listening, not wanting to intrude on Scotty and Marcus. After weeks of isolation, it felt oddly intimate to be in a house with other people,
to know that they were moving around, having conversations, cooking and listening to music.

I heard the wind chime again. And then the soft clink
of porcelain, the sound of running water from the kitchen.
Stepping into the hallway, I followed it to the staircase and
descended to the foyer. The wood floors were cool under
my bare feet. It reminded me that I was wearing boxer
shorts and a tank top. I debated whether to turn around
and change.

"I thought I heard you coming down the stairs." Scotty had spoken softly, but I still jumped a little. "Come into the kitchen. Coffee's on."

I looked down again. "Maybe I should change?"

He smiled. "Don't be silly. We've both seen pajamas."

I swallowed hard at the *we*. That meant Marcus was awake, and I wasn't sure I was ready to face the music.

"Grace," Scotty said gently, "it's fine. Really."

We made our way down the first-floor hall to the kitchen. Marcus was sitting at the island with what looked like a Bloody Mary in front of him.

"Well, well, well," he said. "Sleeping Beauty has awoken."

I listened for the sound of sarcasm in his voice and couldn't find it.

"Good morning." I slid onto one of the stools.

Scotty poured me a cup of coffee. "You could probably use this," he said.

I took it gratefully and inhaled the earthy scent before taking a drink. "Thank you."

He nodded and started pulling pans from the cupboard.

Marcus stood, drink in hand. "Let's go, kid. Time to feed the birds."

I stood uncertainly and followed him toward the open French doors leading to the deck. I cast a glance back at Scotty. He smiled his encouragement.

Marcus began whistling, then singing a carefree tune as he set his drink down and approached a big wooden container on the deck.

I can live in luxury
'Cause I've got a pocketful of dreams

My nervousness grew as he continued to sing. The song was cheerful, too cheerful, and I stood near the outdoor table, still holding my coffee, waiting for him to lower the boom. When he rose from the container, he held a plastic cup full of birdseed and a small silver pouch.

He glanced back at me, the tune waning on his lips. "Well, come on, kid! The birds are hungry!" He looked meaningfully at the container near his feet.

"You want me to help?" I asked.

"Now you're catching on. There's another cup. Grab a scoop and let's go."

I set my coffee down on the table and scooped birdseed out of the container. Then I followed him down the stairs and onto the lawn.

Marcus approached one of the big oak trees along the fence. He handed me his cup. "Hold this."

He reached behind the tree and pulled out a folding step stool, then climbed to the top of it and lifted his arms toward a slim red feeder hanging from one of the branches. I remembered watching him, whistling as he filled the bird feeders next door, from my bedroom window at the house on Camino Jardin.

"It's for the hummingbirds," he explained as he tipped the silver pouch into the top of the feeder. I watched as the clear liquid inside it slowly rose to the top. "They like sugar water. Some people put red dye in it. Hummingbirds like red, you see. But they don't need something fake like dye to be attracted. Anything red will do, even a simple ribbon tied to the feeder."

He stepped down and took his plastic cup from my hand, advancing a few feet down the lawn while holding the step stool in his other hand. He set it down in front of another tree. "Your turn."

I looked up, spotting the bird feeder nailed to the tree. "What do I do?"

"Climb up, dump some of the seed in. That's all there is to it."

I stepped onto the stool and climbed to the top, stretching to reach the feeder. I had just filled it when I caught a scrap of blue and yellow through the trees. I froze, trying to find it again in the dense green foliage.

"Parrot," Marcus pronounced. "There are three that seem to live around this house. I'd gotten friendly with the ones on Camino Jardin, but I'm still working on these fellas."

I'd lost the bird in the branches above my head, and I stepped down, still holding my half-full cup of birdseed. "How do you know which ones are which?" I asked.

He picked up the stool and moved to the back of the lawn. "You get a feel for them," he said. "At first, they all seem the same. Green bodies, a little red near the face. But when you get a better look at them, you see there's more there than meets the eye: a smattering of blue feathers on the underside of a wing, a little orange on the breast. Then you notice their personalities. Some of them are shy and hang back while the others eat first. Some are bold and will try to come after the seed while I'm still filling the feeder. There's one here with a yellow ring around its eyes, likes to scare Scotty, dive-bomb him while he's sitting on the deck with his coffee."

I couldn't help laughing. "Really?"

Marcus flashed a rakish smile. "Really. I think the damn thing knows Scotty's a little afraid of them. I have to try not to laugh."

I smiled, and he indicated the stool. I filled the next feeder, already more comfortable with the process. We were working our way up the other side of the lawn when he spoke again. "You're sure you haven't told anyone about Scotty and me?" he asked. "It's okay if you did. We just need to know what we're dealing with."

"I didn't. I told Selena that I had dinner with friends the other night, but she knows I'm used to taking the bus. I could have meant anyone, could have gone anywhere."

He nodded slowly. "Then we have nothing to worry about, even if Logan does go to the police, and I don't think he will."

I chewed the inside of my cheek. "What makes you so sure?"

We reached the end of the lawn, and he used the step stool to reach the feeder hanging from one of the branches. "If he'd wanted you to go to jail," he started, continuing as he tipped the seed into the top of the feeder, "he would have called the police with the tip that you might be at Selena

Rodriguez's house. He wouldn't have risked confronting you and having you disappear."

"Why do you think he did that?" I asked.

"Well," Marcus said, stepping down onto the grass, "my hunch is that he wants answers. He wants to know why. Or he thinks he does, anyway."

"What do you mean?"

We started toward the deck, our cups empty. "Most of the time when people ask you to explain yourself, they don't really want to hear the answer. What they really want is to hear something that justifies their currently held opinion."

"What do you think is Logan's currently held opinion of me?"

He spoke without hesitation. "That you're a terrible person. That only a really terrible person could do what you did."

"Well, he's right," I said softly.

Marcus stopped walking, and the force of his gaze caused me to stop, too. "It's not that simple, Grace. Life—and people—are all gray area. It's too easy to say all that matters is what we do, that it speaks for itself. But it's not true." He draped an arm around my shoulder as we stepped up to the deck. "We're all works in progress, kid. The things we do are a reflection of our reality at the time. We make mistakes, we learn a little, we correct as we go. You made decisions with the information you had—the situation you had—at the time. That doesn't make you a bad person. It just makes you human. I suspect Logan knows that. If he was so sure you were a bad person, he'd want you in jail, and he would have called the police before looking for you. I'm all for personal responsibility, but what Cormac and Renee did to you and Parker was wrong. Don't be in too much of a hurry to point the finger at yourself that you let them off the hook." He picked up his Bloody Mary glass and finished it, then rattled the ice. "Fuck. I get too philosophical when I drink these things. Should have stuck with coffee."

I laughed, and he ruffled my hair on the way into the house.

Twenty-Six

Scotty and I were heading to the Galleria later that day when I spotted another poster, this one stapled to the bus shelter in front of the Town Center, informing Playa Hermosa residents about the upcoming town meeting. I read it as we drove past, wondering if I would be around to see the outcome.

"People are such assholes sometimes," Scotty said. I turned to look at him, and he raised an eyebrow over his sunglasses. "The peacocks?"

"Do you think they'll get kicked out?" I asked.

"Hard to say," he said. "It's a battle of wills between the people who think they're above anything that makes them uncomfortable and the ones who fancy themselves eco-friendly because it's cool. If you ask me, most of the people in this place couldn't find their way out of a paper bag unless the GPS was working on their Mercedes."

I laughed even though I knew they weren't all like that. "What do you think?" I asked him.

"I think the peacocks were here first," he said. "But that's never counted for much."

I nodded sadly.

He turned left at a fork in the road and headed for PCH. Somehow I wasn't surprised he'd want to take the long way to the mall. It's what I'd always done, and I remembered Selena laughing, teasing that I was so enamored with the ocean that I'd add twenty minutes to our drive just so I could look at the water on the way.

I still wasn't sure why we were going to the mall. Marcus had said he had a line on something that might help us, and Scotty had jumped at the chance to keep me busy, claiming he was claustrophobic from the last two days of cloud cover. We were halfway to the mall when I figured out his secret agenda.

"I want you to think about what you need," he said. "You can't keep wearing the same two outfits over and over."

My cheeks felt hot. "I don't need anything. I'm fine, really. But thank you."

He stopped at a red light and looked at me as he took off his sunglasses. "Are you really going to deprive me of the chance to buy something for someone that doesn't involve birds or tropical flowers?"

I smiled. "I appreciate it. I just . . . You and Marcus have already been too good to me."

Something sad touched his eyes. "What makes you think anything could be too good for you?"

I shook my head. "I . . . I don't know."

He turned his eyes back to the road as the light changed to green. "Well, maybe you should think about that, because I don't think anything's too good for you, and neither does Marcus." He glanced over at me. "But it doesn't matter what we think, now does it?"

I turned my face to the window, my throat closing around the emotion that suddenly rose there.

We arrived at the mall and headed inside, Scotty regaling me with stories about shopping with Marcus. According to Scotty, Marcus's uniform only changed when the temperature dropped below sixty degrees. Then he would trade his cargo shorts for chinos. He had Hawaiian shirts in every color and pattern imaginable, and he had a near-psychic intuition if one of them went missing.

"So I took the green one out of rotation," Scotty was saying as we entered the mall, "rolled it up and tucked it in the back of my sock drawer. My eyes were starting to bleed. And would you believe he came downstairs wearing it the very next day?"

I laughed. I don't know what was funnier to imagine, the look of satisfaction on Marcus's face or Scotty's surprise.

"We need a warm-up," Scotty announced, leading the way to the second floor.

I had no idea what he was talking about, but I followed him past several stores until we came to an arcade. Lights flashed, electronic music and voices spilling from inside the darkened space. Scotty turned into the storefront, stopping when he saw that I was lagging behind.

"Don't tell me you don't like video games," he said.

"No, I do. I just . . ."

"Didn't think I'd like them?" he smiled. "Don't get too confident. I will totally kick your ass at DDR."

He got change from the machine and proceeded to beat me in three games of Dance Dance Revolution. I was sweating by the time we were done, but he looked like he'd been sitting in the shade, enjoying an umbrella drink. He wasn't even breathing hard.

"Need a break?" he asked with a satisfied smirk.

I shook my head, still catching my breath. "Let's just make the next one a sitting-down game."

He grinned. "Deal."

We played a racing game (I finally beat him after four tries) and then moved onto an old-fashioned pinball machine. By the time we finished, we were tied.

"I'll get you on the tiebreaker next time," he said.

We were leaving the arcade when Scotty stopped cold. "Oh, yes. We are definitely doing that."

I followed his gaze to the photo booth, its dingy blue curtain half open to reveal an unoccupied stool. I shook my head. "I can't . . . I don't . . ."

"What?" He looked legitimately confused.

"It's one of the rules. We don't take pictures."

He took my hand. "Well, *we* do." He sighed, and I could

tell that he was struggling to find the right words. "Listen, Grace. I'm not a fan of Marcus's former business endeavors, but there's a right way to do things and a wrong way. You can't live like a ghost, caring about people only because you need them for a job, forgetting about them as soon as you leave, never taking pictures. . . . That's all the stuff that makes life fun. Getting attached and falling in love and making friends and taking pictures." I looked around, wondering if anyone could hear what Scotty was saying, if anyone even cared. But the sound of the arcade muffled everything else, and even if it didn't, what would people hear? Scotty talking about a job that could be anything. Talking about life. I turned back to him as he continued. "You might as well be dead. And you have your whole life in front of you with lots of friends to make and boys to fall in love with and pictures to take. Try to be excited about that. Don't let the past dictate the way you live from here on out. There's no limit to how many times you can reinvent yourself you know."

I nodded and let him lead me into the photo booth. We took two sets of pictures, making goofy faces and vamping for the camera. When the two strips came out of the little slot on the outside of the machine, Scotty handed me one.

"The first of many pictures you'll have to remember the good times."

The words scared me, like they were some kind of jinx against a future that didn't involve jail or the con.

Scotty asked me which stores I liked as we left the arcade, but I hadn't been shopping enough in California to really know, so I just picked ones that I hadn't visited with Selena. The tiniest seed of hope had blossomed inside me. I didn't want reminders of the past. Not today.

Scotty was patient while I agonized over what to buy. It had been a long time since I'd chosen anything to wear without a mark or con in mind. I wasn't even sure what I liked, if I even had a style I could call my own. In the end, I got a couple of pairs of shorts, a new pair of capris, two sundresses, and a few tank tops and T-shirts. I thought we were finished after Scotty insisted on a new pair of sandals and tennis shoes, but he led me to Victoria's Secret instead.

My face got hot as he handed me his credit card. "Honey, don't be embarrassed. Believe me, I can appreciate the importance of nice underwear, even if it's not something I'll ever see Marcus wearing." I burst into laughter at the image as he continued. "Just get what you need. I'm going to sit out here and check my email. Or play Candy Crush. I'll never tell which." He walked away before I could protest.

I bought new underwear and three new bras, then left the store and looked around for Scotty. He was nowhere in sight. My breath caught in my throat, the familiar tingling sensation hitting my head as things started to blur around me. I hurriedly scanned the benches for Scotty as my vision started to cloud. I didn't see him, and everything suddenly got worse, my vision blackening at the edges. I was feeling for the railing that looked down on the first floor of the mall, hoping to brace myself, when Scotty came into view. Concern washed over his face when he saw me, and he pressed a button on his phone and hurried over.

"Grace? What's wrong?" He took my arm and led me to one of the benches. "Deep breaths . . . come on, just keep breathing." He breathed with me, and I tried to slow down to match his breaths. A couple of minutes later, my head started to clear, and my face didn't feel quite as numb. "Better?" he asked.

I nodded. "Better."

"What happened?" he asked.

"I don't know. I came out of the store, and I didn't see you. . . ." It was the first time I'd made the connection. Did I think that Scotty had left me? That I was alone all over again?

"Oh . . . oh, Grace. I'm so sorry." He put an arm around my shoulders and pulled me to him. "I just went into the stationery store across the way to get you this."

I looked down at the bag in his hand. "What is it?"

"There's only one way to find out," he said.

I looked inside and saw only tissue paper. I stuck my hand into the bag and felt past the tissue to something flat and hard. When I pulled it out I saw that it was some kind of notebook or journal, its cover adorned with green-and-blue paisley.

"It's nothing big," Scotty explained. "I just thought it might be nice for you to have a place to write down your thoughts. I do it myself from time to time. I think the reader-writer thing is kind of connected, and since you're a reader, too . . ."

I didn't know what to say. It wasn't just the journal that

choked me up—it was permission to leave proof that I was real.

I looked up at him. "Thank you, Scotty. Really. I love it."

"Good!" His expression grew serious again. "I want you to know something, Grace: Marcus and I are going to see you through this. If you look and don't see me, I'm probably buying a smoothie, okay?"

I nodded, embarrassed at the tears leaking from my eyes. "Thanks."

"Whew!" he said, standing. "I think what really happened is that you almost fainted from hunger! I'm starving. Let's go eat."

We were heading for a little bistro in the mall when my cell phone buzzed. My heart stuttered when I saw that it was a text from Selena. I wasn't sure I was ready for news about Logan, about what he was going to do with the knowledge that I was in Playa Hermosa.

I looked at my phone.

Talked to Logan. He'll give you until Parker's trial date to find Cormac. If you don't do it by then, he's going to turn you in.

And then: **I'm sorry. It's the best I could do.**

I exhaled a breath I didn't know I'd been holding and texted back: **You're sorry? You saved my life. Literally. Thank you. <3**

I put the phone back in my bag and looked at Scotty. "Logan's giving me until June twenty-ninth, Parker's trial date, to turn Cormac in."

"That's great news!" Scotty said. "See? Sometimes you

just have to have a little faith that the universe knows what it's doing, even if it doesn't always make sense when we're in the middle of it."

I nodded, forcing a smile. I knew I should be happy. Logan wouldn't turn me in. At least not right away. What more had I expected? That he would suddenly forgive me? That he would want to see me again? I had no right to expect any of that.

On the way home, we stopped at a bookstore called Pages in Manhattan Beach. I sat on the floor, checking out the backs of books, opening them up to random chapters and reading a few paragraphs the way I'd always liked to do. I felt wrapped in warmth, safely ensconced in a cocoon of books with Scotty nearby. We'd been there an hour when Scotty insisted I pick out a couple to take home with me.

"Marcus will be busy with his part of the work for a few days," he said. "You'll need something to do. Besides watch bad TV with me, I mean."

I reluctantly handed over two books. Scotty paid and we headed back up PCH toward the peninsula and a place that was rapidly beginning to feel like home.

Twenty-Seven

I spent the next ten days reading and sleeping, taking breaks to help Scotty cook or to sit on the big sofa in the living room and watch TV with him. A couple of times I walked in on him facing the wall and sitting in the lotus position on the cushion in the living room. A coil of smoke rose from the incense burner at his side, the scent of sandalwood stronger than normal. I knew he was meditating, and I walked quietly out of the room without saying anything.

Marcus locked himself in his office for hours, appearing in the kitchen only for meals and refills on his coffee. I wasn't sure what he was doing, but I knew it had something to do with the leads I'd provided about Cormac's whereabouts. I heard his voice, muffled through the closed door on the second floor, at all hours of the day and night, and I assumed he was on the phone.

After a few practice runs, I got the hang of feeding the birds, and Marcus let me take over. I'd come to like the morning ritual, and every two or three days I'd take my juice outside, grab the nectar and seed from the big container, and make the rounds. Then I'd sit at the table on the deck and watch the birds flock to the feeders. There were a few that only showed up sporadically, but also three parrots and two hummingbirds that were there every morning. The parrots looked a lot alike, but Marcus was right: it didn't take long to start telling them apart. There was the one with yellow rings around its eyes (it never bothered me, but Marcus hadn't been kidding: it liked to torture Scotty), and another with a green body, its head covered in bright red feathers that continued partway down its back like a cloak. The shiest of the bunch was almost entirely green, the edges of its wings barely touched with blue. The hummingbirds were unique, too: one of them had a chest of brilliant violet, and the other one was covered in iridescent feathers that made me think of Playa Hermosa's peacocks. Their wings beat so fast sometimes that they seemed to be hovering in midair. It felt good to take care of something else, to do something without expecting anything in return, even if it was only for the birds that populated Marcus's lush backyard.

Marcus didn't cook unless it involved slapping meat on the grill, so when Scotty didn't feel like making dinner, we'd order takeout pizza or Thai from the Town Center. Still nervous about being recognized, I never went with Marcus or Scotty to pick it up. I slept more than I thought possible, and often at odd hours of the day. I'd doze on the couch, still clutching my book after breakfast. I'd go to my room to read after lunch and wake up hours later to the sounds of Scotty in the kitchen starting dinner. Once I even fell asleep sitting on the deck, a soft sea breeze blowing in off the water, the crashing of waves against the cliffs below mingling with the chirping of the birds in a kind of lullaby. Scotty waved away my apologies, and after a while, I stopped feeling like I had to offer them.

About a week after my trip to the mall with Scotty, Selena texted me to say she was going to visit Parker. I was nervous about meeting in person to discuss it, but I wanted to see her, and I wasn't crazy about the idea of leaving the details of her meeting with Parker up to chance. She wasn't used to being careful, and I didn't want her to give away the fact that I was in town in case anyone was listening in on the visit. Plus, I'd be lying if I said I wasn't hoping for information on Logan.

Scotty's eyes shaded with worry when I told him I was going to meet Selena at the cliffs. "Are you sure that's a good idea?" he asked. He was standing in the dining room with a spouted metal can in his hand, watering the plants that were scattered around the house. "What about that detective, Fletcher?"

"I can't stay locked up all the time," I said. "I'm getting cabin fever. Besides, I need to give Selena tips for talking to Parker, ways she can let him know I'm trying to get him out without actually saying that I'm in town," I said. "Plus, she's doing this for me. I want to thank her in person."

"How do you know she'll come alone?" he asked.

Was it naive to be sure that she would? I didn't think so. I trusted her, for better or worse. "I just do. She could have turned me in a long time ago."

There was a long pause, and I knew Scotty was thinking, weighing my arguments. "Okay, but I'm going to drive you. That way I can make sure the coast is clear while you meet."

I didn't like the idea of Scotty waiting like a sitting duck. I trusted Selena, but trusting her with my safety was totally different than trusting her with Scotty's, who would be charged with aiding and abetting a criminal—or something like that—if anyone found out he and Marcus were helping me.

"I don't know. . . ."

"Grace, I'm going." His tone told me there was no point arguing. "I'll wait in the car on the road. I just want to make sure she's alone."

I hesitated, trying to come up with another argument. Finally, I nodded. "Okay, if you're sure."

"I am. When are you meeting her?"

"Tonight at seven thirty at the cliffs." I didn't tell him that Selena said couples went there at night to make out, which is why we'd decided to meet between the sunset and postparty hours.

He nodded. "We'll leave at seven."

Twenty-Eight

"Are you nervous?" Scotty asked as we wound our way up the peninsula later that night, following the directions Selena had texted me.

"Kind of," I said. "But only because I want to know about Parker." I looked out the window, the ocean stretching to infinity under the sun, setting in soft shades of orange and pink. "It feels like forever since I've seen him."

"You love him," Scotty said. "And he must love you very much, too. Otherwise he'd be cooperating with the DA. Maybe that's the good thing."

I glanced over at him. "What good thing?"

He slowed down and pulled into a turnout at the side of the road. "I don't know . . . I always feel like something good comes out of everything, even the shitty stuff. Maybe it's because I believe in some kind of underlying order to chaos.

Either that or I'm just naive. But maybe you and Parker finding each other is the one good thing that came from your time with Cormac and Renee." He turned off the car and reached for his door. "Let's take a look before Selena gets here."

We ducked under a cut piece of chain-link fence. It was just like the one Parker and I had used to access another stretch of cliff one misty November morning when we'd finally reached a truce about the Fairchild job. Parker had wanted me to leave with him, to bail on Cormac and Renee and start over somewhere. But I had refused, using the fact that we were family as an excuse to stay together even while we lied and stole from good people, even while we were coming undone at the seams. Now Parker was in prison, and I wished I could go back to that day. Wished I could change my mind, agree to leave with him then and there. If I had, Logan's dad would still be okay, and Parker would be free.

I sometimes forgot that Scotty had been a cop, but I saw it in him as we stepped over the dry brush leading to the edge of the cliff. His eyes were watchful, and there was a practiced caution to his steps, like he was prepared for someone to jump out at us but didn't want to scare me by letting me know he expected it.

It took less than five minutes to reach the edge. Far beyond it, the water was calm. There were hardly any whitecaps, but waves still crashed against the base of the cliffs, the solid wall of rock breaking up their momentum, sending them back out to sea. The wind blew hard and fast, forcing the long grass sideways and sneaking up into my jacket, billowing and snapping with the force of it.

We scanned the overgrown brush for signs of disturbance. When we didn't find any, Scotty stepped closer to the ledge, peering over it, trying to look casual when I knew he was looking for some kind of tactical SWAT team that might be suspended from the cliffs, lying in wait for me. I was almost flattered. As scared as I was of being caught, of being put in jail before I could help Parker, I didn't think I was important enough for the police to deploy cliff-climbing, gun-toting badasses to come after me. Then again, Scotty was the expert.

"Looks good," he finally said, stepping back from the edge. His face was hard and too still, almost unrecognizable from the Scotty I was used to, the one who cooked and watered plants and chided Marcus for drinking straight out of the orange juice container. "I'm going to double back a bit, park on the road so I can keep an eye on everyone who's coming and going." He met my eyes. "If anything looks out of line, I'll come running. Otherwise, text me when you're done."

I could only nod as he gave me a quick squeeze good-bye. I watched him go, his words echoing through my mind: *If anything looks out of line, I'll come running.* It was the complete opposite of Cormac and Renee's strategy, where if you got caught, you were on your own, instructed not to out the family; you were prepared for the fact—not the possibility, the *fact*—that no one was coming to help you. Scotty was willing to put the spotlight on himself, to risk the anonymity he and Marcus had built, to help me. I wasn't really sure what to do with that.

About five minutes after Scotty left, I heard the sound of dirt crunching behind me. When I turned around, I spotted Selena making her way across the brush. Her long hair was tied back in a ponytail that whipped around her face in the wind, and I recognized the slouchy sweater wrapped tightly around her body as one that had belonged to her mother.

"Hey," she said when she reached me.

"Hey."

She gazed at the water below us. "It's windy."

I nodded.

"Want to sit?" she asked.

I looked around, but she seemed to be alone, and even from a distance, I felt Scotty's presence, a life raft in the tumultuous sea of my life. I sat down and Selena dropped to the ground next to me. She tucked her knees up under the sweater and hugged them to her chest.

"I'm sorry about Logan. If I'd known, I would have warned you."

"It's not your fault. You gave me a place to stay, and I appreciate that." I sighed, trying to banish the memory of Logan crying, the sobs that broke free from his throat and the pain in his voice when he asked me if I knew what I'd done to his family. "I just don't get how he was even suspicious."

Selena looked away. "Logan and I have gotten . . . close

since you left." I leaned away from her instinctively, my mind reeling, and she hurried to clarify. "Not like that! It's just . . . we were the closest to you. Everyone else—Olivia, Harper, Liam, David, Raj—they were surprised, maybe even a little hurt, but . . ."

She trailed off, and I filled in the blanks. "But not like you and Logan."

She nodded. "It was hard. No one wanted to talk about it, especially after Logan's dad was checked into Shady Acres. I think they were afraid that it would upset Logan. But he needed to talk about it, and so did I. So we became friends. Really great friends. He was there for me when I was lost, and I like to think I was there for him, too." She shook her head. "Anyway, we know each other pretty well now. In fact, I'd say he knows me better than anyone ever has, except maybe you." She gave me a sad smile.

"So he just . . . had a feeling?" I asked.

"He said I was acting weird, hurrying to get home, spacing out at lunch. . . . Then we were in the library studying for the government final, and I had to go to the bathroom. He looked at my computer and saw that I'd been researching visitation procedures for LA County Jail." She shrugged. "He took a guess. And he apologized for snooping, but I couldn't be mad. We weren't supposed to have secrets. After everything that happened, it was the one rule of our friendship. And I broke it."

"Because of me," I said angrily, pulling at the grass under my fingertips, throwing it to the wind.

"Not everything is your fault, Grace," she said. "I made a choice. And even though Logan was upset, I'd do it again. You needed help. I'm glad I could give it to you, even if it didn't work out."

"Are you guys okay?" I asked. "Is he still pissed at you?"

She sighed. "Yes and no. He's upset, but I really think it's just leftover hurt. He understands why I would want to help you. Why I still care about you."

I wasn't prepared for the admission, and I suddenly didn't want it. Selena still cared about me because that was what Cormac and Renee had taught us: to bond with people under false circumstances, to get them to attach to us in ways that would make them loyal when normal people would question and doubt. The fact that Selena had risked her friendship with Logan to help me was just more evidence that I had been too good at my job. I stood up, suddenly angry under the weight of Selena's caring. "Well, you shouldn't."

"I can't help it, Grace." She laughed a little. "Believe me, I've tried."

I looked away. "Because you're a good person."

"And you're not?" She shook her head. "I'm starting to think it's not that simple." She stood, brushing grass and dirt off her jeans. "Want to talk about Parker?"

I nodded.

"I have a visit scheduled for Saturday. Is that okay?"

"That's great," I said. "Was it hard to set up?"

"Not at all. I was able to do it online."

"Seriously?" I don't know why it surprised me.

She smiled. "Yeah. It was really easy. The only thing is, I had to agree to a video visit to get the Saturday slot. Otherwise it would have taken longer. Apparently there are too many inmates in County Jail and not enough visiting rooms."

"Wait . . . you mean like Skype?"

She shrugged. "I guess. It just gave me the option to check in-person visit or video visit. I tried in-person first, but the first available date was a month from now. I figured you'd want me to get in there sooner than that."

"Definitely. Thank you," I said. "So will you do it from home, or . . . ?"

She shook her head. "There's a place I have to go to where the terminals are set up. But don't worry, I've got it worked out; I'm telling my dad that I'm going to Long Beach to watch Olivia compete in volleyball sectionals. That should cover me for the day."

"Are you sure you want to do this? I know it's a lot to ask. I'll understand if you're not up for it."

"It's no big deal. Just a little drive downtown and a few minutes in front of a computer. Now, if they wanted to strip-search me, we might be having a different conversation."

I couldn't help laughing. "Fair enough."

"So what should I say?" she asked.

I thought about it. It was a no-brainer that video visits would be monitored, so whatever Selena said had to sound boring, like the same stuff anyone else would talk about when visiting someone in jail. "You should try to sound casual, natural, like you're just an old friend paying him a visit. Don't use my name; don't say anything about me. You won't have to worry about Parker's end of the conversation; he would never say anything to compromise his trial."

"Okay, but if I don't use your name, how will he know you're trying to help him?" she asked. "Isn't that the whole point?"

"We just have to think of a way to let him know that no one else will understand." I searched my memory for the jobs we'd done together, the lies we'd told. "I know—tell him you ran into Bailey, from DC."

"Bailey?"

I nodded. "She was one of Parker's marks in Baltimore. Her parents joked that she and I looked so much alike that we could have been sisters."

"And he'll know what I mean?" Selena asked.

"I think so."

"Okay, then what?"

"Tell him . . ." I paused, trying to think of a way to let Parker know that I was nearby, that I was going to get him out, without giving myself—or Selena—away. "Tell him you ran into Bailey from DC and she said she can't wait to see you, and she hopes it'll be soon."

"Bailey from DC," Selena muttered. "She can't wait to see you, hopes it'll be soon." She looked at me. "I can do that."

"Great. Thank you so much, Selena. Really."

"It's no big deal. To be honest, I feel kind of bad that I

haven't thought to visit him before."

"You feel *bad*?"

"I know," she said, "it sounds crazy. But I never really thought about why you and Parker might have done it. I mean, I *thought* about it. But it never occurred to me that maybe you didn't want to, that maybe you were being used by Cormac and Renee." She held up a hand to stop me when I started to say something. "And I know you say it was your choice, and that you have to take responsibility for your part of it. I even agree with those things. But I don't know." She sighed. "I guess I can see where you might have gotten . . . confused about what to do and how to handle things."

"Well, just so you know, I'm not nearly as forgiving of myself as you're being," I said. "And for the record, Parker wanted me to run with him before we took Warren's gold."

"Why didn't you?"

"I don't know. I feel stupid saying it now, but Cormac and Renee were my mom and dad, the only family I'd known. I guess Parker just saw things more clearly."

"That's why he's the big brother," she said.

I laughed a little.

Selena rubbed her arms. "We should go. It's getting dark."

I looked at the horizon, the sun long gone, leaving a gray-violet haze over the water. "I guess so."

We started walking back toward the road.

"Do you need a ride somewhere?" she asked when we reached her car.

"Nah, I'm good."

"Are you sure? Where are you staying?" I bit my lip, and she laughed. "Got it. Can you at least tell me if you're okay? If you have everything that you need?"

"I do," I said, surprised to find that for the first time in a long time, I meant it.

Now I just needed to get Parker.

Twenty-Nine

I was sitting on a stool in the kitchen a couple of days later, Scotty knuckle deep in the foam on my head, when Marcus emerged from his office.

"Jesus!" he said, pretending I'd scared him. "What happened to your hair?"

"Ha-ha. Very funny," I said. "My roots were showing. Scotty's helping me touch up the color."

Marcus nodded, pouring himself a glass of wine. "What color is it? When you're not incognito, that is?"

It had been so long since I'd worn my natural color that I had to think about it. "Dirty-blondish, I guess? Like, dark blond?"

Marcus squinted a little as he studied my face, like he was trying to imagine the hair color on me. "You know what, kid? I think you'd look just as good with any color hair. Not that I know hair. Or teenage girls."

His voice had gone a little gruff, and I smiled at the roundabout compliment. When I looked up at Scotty, his hands coated with foam, he was smiling, too.

"Anyway," Marcus said, clearing his throat. "I have a job for you."

"For me?"

He nodded. "If you're feeling up to it."

Scotty took his hands off my head. "Let it sit for a bit and then we'll rinse."

"Thanks, Scotty." I turned my attention back to Marcus. "I'm up to it. Is it about Cormac?"

He slid onto one of the stools. "Yep."

"Did you find a lead?"

"I'm still working on something solid," he said. "But I used some of the information you gave me about Seattle to narrow the field. Cormac can't use the most reputable fences and ID brokers. They won't touch someone who's as hot as he is right now." I was still getting my head around the fact that there was such a thing as reputable fences and ID brokers when he continued. "That means he'll have to use the people on the bottom rung. Most of them aren't nice people, but he doesn't have a choice."

"And that helped you track him?" I asked.

"It helped me narrow the field, assuming he's still in the Seattle area. And I think he is. Moving would be too expensive."

I grabbed a peach from the basket on the island and bit

into it. "What can I do to help?"

"If Cormac is still in Seattle, I think he's most likely to be in a couple of places: neighborhoods with public transportation, cheap hotels, and close proximity to the bottom rung. Lucky for us, Scotty still has connections with the Seattle PD."

I stopped chewing. "Did someone spot him?"

"Not yet," Marcus said. "But I'm hoping you will."

"I'm confused," I admitted.

"I called in favors with some of the people I know on the force up north," Scotty said. "We got some security footage in the areas Marcus is talking about. It's nothing comprehensive. In fact, it's kind of hit and miss—not every store has video surveillance, and not every street has traffic cameras. But it's something, and it's all we've got."

"You want me to go through the tapes?" I asked. "See if I can spot him?"

"Basically," Marcus said.

"And they're not all tapes," Scotty said. "Some of it's digital footage that I can send to your laptop."

I nodded. "I can do that, but you know Cormac has probably changed his appearance, dyed his hair or something."

"I don't doubt it," Marcus said, "although I'm willing to bet the bastard still looks like himself. Vanity is a killer in this business."

"And anyway," Scotty broke in, "you're still the best person to spot him. Marcus hasn't seen him up close in years."

"That makes sense," I said. After nearly two weeks

sleeping, reading, and stuffing my face with Scotty's cooking, I was suddenly excited to have a job. "When do I start?"

"As soon as you get that stuff out of your hair," Marcus said. "I'll set everything up in the living room."

Thirty

I was sitting on the sofa in the living room Saturday afternoon when my cell phone buzzed. I jumped, digging through the sofa cushions to find it, relieved to see it was a text from Selena.

Done. Want to meet?

I typed back. **When/where?**

I can pick you up in half an hour?

I was 99 percent sure I could trust Selena with my address, but that 1 percent was still an unacceptable risk where Marcus and Scotty were concerned.

I'll meet you somewhere.

K, bus stop at the TC in half an hour?

I'll be there.

I pressed Pause on the remote, and the grainy black-and-white footage froze on the big-screen TV. There was an old woman at the counter, paying for what looked like a carton of cigarettes and a gallon of milk. It had come from a convenience store in a sketchy part of Seattle, but it could have been from any of the locations I'd viewed over the past two days. Liquor stores, minimarts, even a porn store, much to my horror. Scotty had offered to take that one, but I'd kept a straight face and said I'd do it, mostly because imagining Scotty watching footage from a porn store, even to try to find Cormac, was worse than doing it myself.

So far I'd found nothing. There had been one false alarm. A man wearing a too-big suit, his hair receding (could have been prosthetic), large glasses perched on his nose. He looked nothing like Cormac, but there had been something about the way he walked down the aisle of the used-car lot, the arrogant way he held himself, that made me think of the man who had called himself my father. I'd gotten Marcus and Scotty, but after twenty minutes of debate, we'd decided it wasn't Cormac. We'd filed the location away for future reference in case we decided it was worth a second look, and I'd moved onto the next tape.

"Taking a break?" Scotty asked, dropping onto the couch next to me. "We could watch the next episode of *Alias*." We'd been working our way through the old show while Marcus had been holed up in his office.

"Will the offer be open in a couple of hours?" I asked. "Selena texted. She's back from seeing Parker. We're going to meet."

"Of course," he said. "Where are you meeting Selena?"

"At the bus stop in front of the Town Center in about twenty-five minutes," I said. "But I can walk. It's not that far."

Scotty stood. "Not with Fletcher out there. I'll drive you. I have to grab some wine for dinner anyway."

There was enough wine in the kitchen to get us through every dinner for the next ten years, but I didn't say anything. Then I realized that I'd thought about my time with Scotty and Marcus like it would go on forever. Like I would still be here for dinner in ten years, when this was just another temporary rest stop. I stifled the loss that rolled over me like a giant wave. It was too easy to get stuck underneath, to run out of air. I had to keep moving.

I changed out of my yoga pants and met Scotty in the foyer. We took the SUV to the Town Center. Scotty parked, waiting for me to get out.

I turned to him as I reached for the door. "Aren't you going to get the wine?"

He looked a little flustered. "Definitely." He made a show of pulling out his cell phone and looking at the screen. "I just have to text Marcus first."

I tried to hide my smile. "Okay, I'll see you in a couple of hours."

"Text me when you need a ride home," he called as I got out of the car.

When I got to the bus stop, I looked back and spotted Scotty still watching me through the windshield. He hurriedly bent back to his phone.

Fletcher was still out there somewhere, and I stood back

in the bus shelter, pretending to look at my phone while I scanned my surroundings through the shaded lenses of my sunglasses. I'd only been there for a couple of minutes when Selena rolled up in her dad's Cadillac.

I hurried around to the passenger side and got in.

"Hey," she said, pulling back onto the road.

"Hey." I studied her reflection, wondering if it was my imagination that she looked a little pale. "You okay?"

She nodded. "It was just . . . harder than I expected it to be."

I hesitated. The thought that Selena's car might be bugged was paranoid, even for me, but being careful was practically coded in my DNA. I didn't know how to act any other way. "I want to hear all about it," I finally said, "but we shouldn't talk here."

She glanced over, her expression confused. A second later, understanding washed over her features. "Got it." She refocused on the road. "Where we should go?"

"Somewhere outside would be nice," I said.

She seemed afraid to say anything after that, and we drove in silence toward Redondo. She turned into the parking lot that stood over the beach and pier. "Is this good?"

"Perfect."

We got out and headed down the stairs to the strand, then followed it onto the pier. "I'm starving," Selena said. "I was too nervous to eat earlier. Want to grab something?"

"Sounds good," I said.

We walked up to one of the counters serving food and

ordered two cups of clam chowder and two Cokes, then carried everything to a table near one of the pier's railings. The tide was receding, increasing the square footage of the beach every time it rolled back out to sea. There were only a handful of surfers in the water, plus a few people walking along the sand, getting their feet wet as the water rushed onto the beach.

I took a bite of the clam chowder. It was hot, and I had to take a drink of Coke to cool down my mouth before asking Selena the question that had been beating in my mind like a drum since the minute I'd gotten into the car with her.

"How is he?"

She chewed slowly, and I wondered if she was doing it on purpose, if she was trying to find a way to tell me about Parker without freaking me out. A knot started to form in my stomach.

"He's okay, I think." She put her spoon down and sighed. "Honestly? It was kind of hard to tell."

"What do you mean?"

"Just that he looks like Parker—except for the short hair—but there's something different about him, too. He seemed nervous when we first started talking, like he didn't know why I was there."

"He probably thought you'd come to chew him a new one," I said.

"Maybe."

"How was he different?" At first I wasn't sure I even wanted to know, but a second later I knew that I did. That I needed to know. It was the only way I could share this with him. The only way we could really be in it together, like we'd been in everything since the day Cormac and Renee had adopted him.

She seemed to think about it as she took a drink of her soda. "He seems older. More careful."

"Parker's always been careful," I said, remembering his serious eyes, the way he moved, slowly, like he expected life to throw something unexpected at him.

"That's true," she agreed. "But this felt different. Like he was afraid to make any sudden movements, afraid to speak in case he said the wrong thing."

I thought about prison, about what it must be like for Parker there. It hurt so much that my lungs seemed to close. But I made myself imagine it, made myself see it.

"He's in jail," I said softly. "He's probably afraid of all those things and more."

She nodded sadly. "He doesn't belong there, Grace. Even I could see that."

I swallowed against the tears that stung my eyes. "Did he look . . . hurt?"

"He didn't have any bruises or cuts. Nothing like that."

"Well, that's good at least." I put my spoon down, my appetite gone even though I'd only eaten a couple of bites. "What did you guys talk about?"

"Not much. I told him I wanted to see him, to make sure he was okay. He said he appreciated it, but he was fine. I asked him if there was anything he needed. He said no. That kind of thing."

"Did he . . . did he ask about me?"

She shook her head, and I knew it had been a stupid question. Parker wouldn't ask about me. He wouldn't ask Selena if she'd heard from me because he wouldn't want to hear the answer, to risk that she might give something away.

"Did you tell him?" I asked. "What we talked about?"

"Yep. I said it just like you told me: I ran into Bailey from DC the other day. She said to tell you hello, that she hopes to see you soon."

"And?"

She hesitated, like she was remembering. "I think he got it. For a second he looked confused, but then his eyes seemed . . . clearer."

"What did he do?" I was starved for details about him.

"He just kind of nodded, like he understood. And he made eye contact with me. He hadn't up until then."

I exhaled. "Good. Thank you, Selena."

"It's fine," she said. "I should have visited him before now. It . . ." She looked down at her hands.

"I didn't expect that of you. No one did. We're not your responsibility."

"I know, but I'm glad I went. I hope you feel better. I do," she admitted.

I smiled a little. "Me too."

It wasn't entirely true. I was glad Parker knew that I was nearby, that I was trying to help him. But now I could see him in my mind, clad in an orange jumpsuit, moving carefully, not talking for fear of saying the wrong thing, being scared and not having anyone to say that to. That was the worst: having to keep everything inside. Sometimes you just needed to say it, to name your fear, in order to take away some of its power.

"I'm glad," she said. "Is there anything else I can do?"

"No, but thank you."

"Have you made any progress on Cormac and his sources?" she asked.

"Not really." I thought about the security footage. "I have a line on something, but I don't know yet if it'll lead to anything real."

"Will you keep in touch?" she asked. "Let me know if I can help?"

I smiled a little. "Of course."

She looked at her phone. "I should get back. I'm not sure how long I can stretch this volleyball sectionals thing, especially since I have my dad's car."

We talked about Nicaragua on the ride home. Selena was leaving right after school got out and was both nervous and excited. I was flush with happiness for her, and also a little envious. I could see her, out in the jungle somewhere, working on a school or building an orphanage, helping people and growing up and figuring out who she would be in the world.

It was after six o' clock when she dropped me at the bus stop in front of the Town Center. I started walking toward Colina Verde, glad the sun had slipped behind the houses on the peninsula, leaving the sidewalks in perpetual shade. I knew Scotty would come get me if I called, but I needed the time to think about Selena's visit with Parker, to process her observations and put them together with what I knew about him to get a real picture of his state of mind.

I was working my way up the last hill before the turn onto Colina Verde when my eye was drawn to a piece of paper stapled to one of the light posts. I stepped closer, my breath getting more shallow as the photographs on the flyer came into view.

They were pictures of me.

The first one, taken from my Chandler High School ID, showed me smiling, blond, and tan. The second one was a digital rendering, the kind police have to do when they're guessing how someone might look. It showed me with pale skin and dark hair, and I felt suddenly exposed, like every person in every house on the street could tell it was me.

There was a short paragraph under the pictures, and I leaned in to read.

WANTED AS PERSON OF INTEREST

The Playa Hermosa Police Department would like to speak to the above female, Grace Fontaine, 17, in connection with a theft on the peninsula last year. Please contact Detective Fletcher in confidence at 323-555-7491 with any information.

A person of interest? They knew I was nearby, and they knew I'd been involved in the Fairchild theft. They were just trying to make it seem like no big deal so people would feel better about identifying me.

I stepped away, resisting the urge to tear the flyer down, to look for others and take them all down. That would be a mistake. I would only draw attention to myself, make someone who might be passing by or looking out their window wonder why I would bother. I turned away and started walking.

It was hard not to glance around. I felt exposed, like I was walking down a hallway at school while everyone whispered behind my back. I forced myself to move at my normal pace, talking myself down as I made my way to the safety of Scotty and Marcus's house. It was just a picture. It only looked like me because I knew it *was* me. A bystander would never look closely enough to connect the dots, and Selena and Logan had already promised to keep my presence a secret. For now, at least.

I was almost to the corner of Colina Verde and the safety of Scotty and Marcus's house when someone got out of a black BMW parked near the curb. I didn't recognize her. I thought she was just someone who lived on the peninsula. Someone's friend or mother. But then she stopped, took off her sunglasses, said my name, and I knew I'd been right. She was someone's mother.

Mine.

Thirty-One

The blond hair was gone, replaced by a short, swingy chop of black fringe that might have been a wig. Her body was fuller and rounder, not enough to make her overweight, but enough to soften the angular edges she'd taken so much pride in maintaining. Even her clothes were different, the tight jeans and revealing tops she liked to wear between jobs replaced with gray slacks and a black T-shirt.

I don't know how long I stared at her. I was in shock, struck wordless by the unexpected sight of her on the heels of the flyers that were probably plastered all over the peninsula.

"Why don't you get in the car, Grace?" she said. "You've done a good job with the hair and make up, you don't look like yourself at all, but neither of us should risk it."

I was torn between warring impulses. Part of me wanted

to run away from her and never look back. But there were other parts—the eleven-year-old girl who'd been grateful to be adopted, the teenager who'd believed she finally had a mother—that wanted to step toward her, let her stroke my hair and call me Gracie.

I shook my head, like that would shake some sense into it. Renee had betrayed me in a million different ways. Even under the rules of the grift, she'd betrayed me, betrayed all of us, and that wasn't counting the fact that she'd bailed as my mother, had left Parker to rot in jail.

"I have nothing to say to you," I said, turning away.

"I'm sorry, Grace." Something in her voice made me turn around. Some hint of regret or sorrow that I couldn't even be sure was there. Maybe I just wanted it to be there. "I'm so, so sorry. I had no idea things were going to go down the way they did. Please . . . just get in the car and let me explain."

I thought about Parker and the things Selena had told me about him. I would do anything to get him out of jail. Even talk to Renee. Because if I couldn't find Cormac, Renee was a close second. Maybe even better, since she had the gold—or the money she'd traded it for.

I moved toward the car and slid into the passenger seat. Renee closed the driver's-side door, sealing us away from the rest of the world. She took off her sunglasses, and I felt her eyes on my face.

"How are you, Gracie?" she said softly.

My head snapped up. "Don't call me that. Don't ever call me that again."

She nodded, her slim throat rippling as she swallowed hard. "Are you safe? Taken care of?"

"Why are you pretending you care?" I asked. "Just . . . stop pretending. In case you haven't noticed, the game is over. Parker and I lost."

"I'm not pretending," she said. "I've been worried about you. I just needed to set up someplace safe before I came back for you."

"It's a lot harder to con everybody into thinking you're normal when you can't trot out your kids to do all the work for you, isn't it?"

She flinched a little. "I deserve that. But the truth is, I didn't have to come back. I sold the gold just like we planned. I had to take less than I expected, but I'm not hurting for money. I just didn't want to start over without you."

"Without me? What about Parker? What about Cormac? He's an asshole, but he didn't deserve to have you steal his share of the money. To have you leave him high and dry. If you'd wanted out, you could have taken your share and gone. At least then Parker would have had money for a decent lawyer."

"It's not that simple, Grace." I recognized the hard edge to her voice. It was the one she used when we had to do something unpleasant, when there was no way around it. It was her stop-whining-and-get-it-done voice. "Cormac betrayed Marcus. You must know that now, given your current living arrangements."

"How do you—"

"It doesn't matter," she said, interrupting me. "I know. And you have to know that if Cormac did it to Marcus, it was only a matter of time before he did it to me. To us. He was getting distant. We were fighting. The Fairchild job was the perfect opportunity for him to take the money and run."

I thought back to the months leading up to the Fairchild job. Things had been tense between Renee and Cormac, between everyone. "So you beat him to it," I said.

"I did what I had to do," she said. "Like always. And I did it for you and Parker, too. Do you really think if Cormac took the money he'd make sure you got your share?"

"Well, you didn't exactly make sure we got it, did you?" I hated myself for saying it. I didn't care about the money from Warren Fairchild's gold. It was tainted, poisoned by the loss it had caused Logan and his family, by the sadness Selena now wore like a shroud, by Parker's imprisonment. But it was just another blow from Renee, another way she had abandoned me.

"I have it set aside for you," she said, "just like we planned."

"You expect me to believe you'll just hand it over? Write Parker a check for his legal defense? Write me one for college?"

"It's not that simple, Grace, and you know it. If I give you money for Parker's lawyer, where will Parker say he got it? How will you explain it?" She narrowed her eyes at me. "Besides, you seem to have a plan of your own."

Somewhere in the part of my mind that wasn't blinded

by rage, I knew she was right, but her reference to my plan—
to Marcus—caused a fresh flood of anger through my veins.
"I didn't have a choice. And the fact that I managed to come
up with a way to help Parker doesn't mean you're off the
hook for helping him, especially since you have his money."

She turned her palms up. "What do you expect me to
do? How can I help in a way that won't compromise you or
Parker? That won't compromise me?"

It was a question without an answer, which was the only
reason she was asking it. And then I realized there was an
answer. There was one thing she could do.

"You could turn yourself in," I said. "Trade yourself for a
reduced sentence for Parker and me."

"Grace." She said it softly, almost like she was dis-
appointed I would even suggest it, that I would even go
through the motions of making her say no. "You know I
can't do that."

I turned angrily toward her. "Can't or won't?"

"Both," she said simply. "I'm not willing to give up my
freedom and the money we worked so hard for when there's
every possibility Parker will go free anyway, especially with
you and Marcus working together. If I gave myself up, none
of us would have access to the money. We'd be sacrificing
something we don't need to sacrifice to achieve an end that's
achievable through other means. It doesn't make good business sense."

"I could just turn you in," I said.

She smiled sadly. "You don't have enough information

to do that. Besides, I think we all know Cormac's the real bad guy in all of this. He would have abandoned all of us, and you can bet your ass he wouldn't have left a thirty-five-thousand-dollar bar of gold like I did. He wouldn't have come back for you like I'm doing. Cormac's all about Cormac. I think you know that by now."

I choked out a bitter, hard laugh. "And you're some kind of Mother Teresa?"

She met my eyes. "No, Grace. I know what I am. I always have. But I also know what I'm not. I would never have bailed on Marcus the way Cormac did, but Marcus wasn't my partner. It wasn't my decision to make. I only did what I did after the Fairchild job because I knew Cormac was getting ready to do it to me. Protecting myself doesn't make me a bad person."

"It does when it comes at everyone else's expense," I said, reaching for the door.

"Wait, Grace. Just . . . wait." She took a deep breath. "I'm set up somewhere. Somewhere quiet and safe. You can come with me. We can wait for Parker. We can even get you a good ID, the last one you'll need, I promise. You can go to college, do all the things you always wanted to do. We can leave right now."

I didn't even have to think about it. "I'm not leaving Parker. Not ever again."

She looked down at her lap. "I can stay nearby for a while, but not for long. You can join me after you find Cormac, after you get Parker out. We can all start over. I . . . ." Her voice broke a little. "I was . . . hard on you. Cormac was so god-damn militant. It didn't leave room for anything human. But I love you. I know I didn't do a good job of showing you, but you're my daughter, and I love you. You should be with me."

My resolve started to crumble under the weight of the words I'd waited for her to say. "How could I ever trust you again?" I asked.

She exhaled. "I don't know, Grace. I guess we'll just have to start over. But we can't do that if you don't let me in, if you don't give me a second chance."

"I don't know if I can," I said, getting out of the car.

"Grace, wait!" she called before I could shut the door. "Will you think about it? Try to remember the good times and at least think about it?"

I wanted to say no, to shut the door and walk away. But that would mean never seeing her again, and now that she was in front of me, I longed for the days when she'd smooth back my hair while we watched a movie, the times we laughed trying on clothes we hated to work a job, the way we'd planned our girls' trip to Paris, the one we never got to take. It was stupid and crazy, but I couldn't help it. Besides, where would I go when I got Parker out of jail? I had no money, no friends, no family. Parker wouldn't want to set-tle down, and I was tired of moving around all the time. I wanted a home, one place that was mine. Where would I have that if not with Renee?

"Give me your number," I said. "Or some way to reach you. I'll think about it."

She shook her head. "I can't do that, but if you give me yours, I'll check in with you in a few days."

She was afraid I'd turn her in, worried that I'd give her number to the police, that they might be able to use it to track her. I didn't blame her. She had more to lose than I did. I'd already lost everything.

I gave her the number and walked away.

Thirty-Two

I was still shaking when I got to Scotty and Marcus's house. I set my bag on the bench by the front door and followed the sound of Scotty's music playing in the living room. He was lying on the sofa, reading, when I came in.

"You're home! I was wonder—" He stopped talking and sat up, setting his book aside. "What's wrong?"

I dropped onto the other end of the couch. I thought I'd feel safe once I was home, but it was like all the fear I'd bottled up on the street had finally been let loose, and I just started shaking harder. Renee was still fresh in my mind, but I hadn't had time to process seeing her, to figure out what it meant for Parker and me. I started with the other stuff instead.

"There are flyers . . . ," I tried to explain.

Scotty shook his head. "What are you saying, Grace?"

I swallowed hard, holding my hands together in my lap,

trying to keep them still. "I was walking home from the bus stop and saw flyers with my picture on them."

"What kind of flyers?" Marcus's voice came from the doorway, and he stepped into the room and sat on one of the chairs opposite the sofa.

"They're calling me a 'person of interest,'" I said. "Asking people to contact Detective Fletcher if they see me on the peninsula."

Marcus leaned forward. "What did the pictures look like? When were they taken?"

I described the photographs to him, careful to be honest about the second one, about how much it would look like me without makeup. Glossing over the truth wouldn't do us any favors in the long run.

Marcus and Scotty exchanged a glance. It was only a split second, but the worry was evident in their eyes before they recovered, composing their faces into matching masks of calm.

"This doesn't have to be a big deal," Marcus said. "You don't leave the house much anyway, and you can always color your hair a different color."

"Exactly," Scotty agreed. "But no more walking around the peninsula. I'll drive you. No one will be able to identify you in the passenger seat of a car."

I stood, pacing the floor, my earlier fear turning to a kind of manic agitation that made me feel like I wanted to crawl out of my skin. "But it means he's close," I said. "Fletcher knows I'm here, and now he's sniffing me out. It's only a matter of time before he finds me."

Scotty rose from the couch and put a hand on my shoulder. He looked into my eyes. "That's not true. He's covering his bases, that's all. It's what any cop would do."

"Castillo didn't do it."

"That's because Castillo wants to help you. Isn't that what you said?" Marcus asked.

"I guess."

Marcus nodded. "This isn't even a close call. Not by my standards. Fletcher's looking for you, yes, but right now all he has is a possible sighting by someone on the peninsula. If they knew for sure you were here, they'd be doing a lot more than putting up flyers."

"Marcus is right," Scotty said. "And I haven't seen an increase in police presence. They're reaching."

I knew they were downplaying the danger to keep me calm, but it didn't work. I felt Fletcher out there, a hunter on the trail of his prey. He couldn't see me yet. But he knew he was close. Still, there was nothing else to say about it. I'd just have to find Cormac before Fletcher found me. It was the only thing I could do.

I sighed. "I guess you're right. I'm sorry I freaked out a little."

Scotty put an arm around me. "It's completely understandable. But try not to worry. We're almost there."

"And on the plus side," Marcus said, "Scotty bought some of that ice cream you like, the one with the cherries and the chocolate?"

I tried to smile. "I feel better already."

I felt a little guilty as we headed to the kitchen. I don't know why I hadn't yet said anything about Renee—common sense dictated that my loyalty lay with Marcus and Scotty now. But protecting Renee was habit, and I was starting to wonder if there would ever be a time when I could be loyal to only myself.

Thirty-Three

A few days later, I drove with Scotty to pick up pizza from the Town Center. I'd wanted to stay home, afraid to be seen at the one place on the peninsula where everyone congregated, but Scotty had handed me a baseball cap and insisted it would be good for me to get out, even if I did have to stay in the car while he ran in for the pizza.

I knew he was right. However much I tried to seem unaffected, Fletcher was never far from my mind. If a car door slammed outside, I hurried to peer though the curtains, convinced the detective was on his way up the walkway to question Marcus and Scotty. If it was too quiet, I was sure the police were getting ready to raid the house. In my dreams I was always running, chased through woods, on the beach, through the winding streets of Playa Hermosa. I woke up breathing fast and heavy, the feel of Fletcher's hand clamped around my arm as real as if he was right there in the guest room. I'd even called Detective Castillo, hoping for something concrete to ease my mind, but he'd only been able to tell me what we already suspected: Castillo was taking the sighting of me seriously, canvassing the peninsula and putting the word out that I was wanted by the police.

"If you've got anything up your sleeve, now would be a good time to pull it out," Detective Castillo had said, as if I was holding back for some kind of dramatic reveal when the truth was, we just didn't have anything on Cormac's whereabouts.

Scotty and I talked about the security footage as we drove to the Town Center. I'd been reviewing it for a week, and I still hadn't seen Cormac. There was the one close call in the used-car lot, but other than that, nothing. I still had a few tapes Scotty had gotten from businesses in the area where Marcus thought we were most likely to find Cormac. After that, I'd have to move on to the traffic surveillance tapes, and I was a lot less optimistic about finding Cormac on those. I wasn't even sure he had a car, and if he did, spotting him while he was doing fifty miles an hour or stopped for a few seconds at a red light seemed unlikely. Marcus was quietly working his own leads, but so far he had nothing to say about them. I figured that probably meant he didn't have anything solid either.

"Don't worry," Scotty said, as if he'd read my mind. He pulled into the parking lot at the Town Center. "Marcus keeps things close to the vest until he's sure he has something. The fact that he hasn't said anything doesn't mean he isn't close."

"I hope you're right," I said. We only had a little over two weeks until Parker's trial date, and I was starting to feel the ticking clock under both of us. If we didn't find some kind of information to help him, he'd go to jail and I'd be back on my own.

"I'm always right. Just ask Marcus." He winked and reached for the door. "You okay here while I go in?"

I nodded. "I'm good."

He shut the door and hurried toward Joey's Real New York Pizza (Selena had once told me Joey was from New Jersey). I turned around in my seat, scanning the shopping center from the safety of the tinted rear window. It was quiet for a Friday night, and I was turning back around when a black limo eased into the parking lot. I twisted farther in my seat to get a better view. Playa Hermosa was home to some of the wealthiest people in Southern California, but a limo at the Town Center was still an anomaly.

The limo came to a stop in front of Mike's. A second later the driver hopped out and hurried to one of the rear doors. He opened it, and a gown-clad woman stepped out of the back. No, not a woman.

Rachel Mercer.

I hardly recognized her with her hair piled in curls on top of her head, her makeup dark and smoky. She was wearing a long violet gown that hugged every long, lean curve, one slender leg emerging from a slit that went halfway up her thigh. She turned, laughing at something someone said behind her, and a moment later Logan emerged from the limo.

My breath caught at the sight of him, looking even more handsome than I remembered in a simple black tux. The flower on his lapel was a deep lilac, leaving no doubt who was his date.

And then I understood: it was prom night. Olivia and Harper had tried to get me to join the committee last fall, but the Fairchild job had been nearing its close, the end of my time with Logan sitting like a lead weight on my chest. I didn't think I'd be in Playa Hermosa all these months later for prom night.

And I wasn't, I reminded myself. Not really. I was just a ghost.

I watched the others get out of the car—Selena wearing a dark green dress, David close at her side. Olivia in short red silk. Harper in white. And all the guys in tuxes, looking older than when I'd last seen them. I wondered what they were doing as they headed into Mike's—stopping for cheese fries on their way to the dance? They disappeared into the burger joint and I turned back around in my seat, watching traffic pass on the main road in front of me. Seeing everyone together, having fun and laughing and heading to prom, should have made me sad. Actually, if I was a good person, it should have made me happy. They deserved this night, especially Selena and Logan.

But I didn't feel either of those things. Instead, a surge

of anger rushed my body like the water at high tide. I was unaccountably mad at them. All of them. They were doing a normal thing, having fun, while I hid in Scotty's car, afraid even to go in to get the pizza. My mind knew it was irrational. They hadn't done anything wrong. I was in this position because of the things I had done. But telling myself that didn't help, and I still felt like a little kid, watching everyone else eat ice cream on the swings while I sat alone in the shadows.

I felt the tightening in my chest, the impending panic attack like an incoming missile. I forced myself to breathe slowly like Scotty had taught me, to blot out everything else as I focused only on my breath, making its way in and out of my nose. By the time Scotty came back, the vise around my chest had loosened its grip, my earlier rage dissipating in a more painful swell of melancholy.

"Apparently, sausage is a vegetable in New York," Scotty said as he handed me the pizza across the center console. "I didn't want to wait for them to make a new one. We can just pick it off."

I took the pizza. "That's fine." I was only vaguely aware that my voice was wooden.

He got in the car and shut the door. "What's wrong?"

I shook my head, and just then, something caught Scotty's eye in the rearview mirror. He turned around in his seat. "Oh . . . Oh, Grace. I'm so sorry."

I chewed my lip as the limo pulled out of the parking lot and onto the road. "It's okay," I said. "It's not like I ever thought I'd be able to go."

"I know," he said, "but seeing it is still harder than imagining it."

I nodded.

He took a deep breath. "You've missed out on a lot, but now you're taking back your life, one step at a time. You can have all of that, honey: dances and boyfriends and college and . . . well, anything. But the first step is getting Cormac."

I turned to him. "What if Fletcher finds me first?" I asked. "What if I . . . go to jail?" I had to beat back my panic at the thought.

"We won't let that happen," Scotty said. "We're going to get Cormac, and we're going to get the best deal we can for you and Parker so you can get the clean slate you deserve. But right now, you have to focus on what's in front of you. Tune out everything else, and just focus on the next thing."

"Trying to find Cormac."

"Exactly," he said.

I nodded, my anger and sadness hardening into resolve. "I can do that."

He turned on the car. "Of course you can. But not on an empty stomach."

Thirty-Four

Two days later I was sitting in the hammock out back with my laptop, looking at the last of the security footage from Seattle. It was a little awkward, getting settled into the swinging contraption while holding my computer, but my brain was fuzzy from all the grainy images I'd reviewed over the past week or so. I'd started to get lazy, tuning out the footage for seconds at a time while I thought about Parker, Logan, Renee. A change of scenery had made all the difference.

I pressed Pause on the video file Scotty had sent me and looked up into the trees, scanning for the parrots. A new one had shown up a couple of days ago. Unlike the regulars, this one was almost entirely blue, with just a little bit of orange under its neck and on its breast. The others didn't know what to do with it. Scotty's yellow-eyed enemy flew around the newcomer squawking, trying to keep it from the

bird feeders, but the others seemed more curious than anything else. I couldn't help wondering if it would stick it out
and stay or get fed up and leave. There were lots of trees in
Playa Hermosa. Lots of places it could go.

A couple of minutes later I saw it approaching the feeder
nearest the deck. It landed on a nearby tree first, looking
around like it was trying to see if the coast was clear. The
other birds were nowhere in sight, and it cautiously flew
to the feeder and took some seed before flying quickly to
another branch. A second later, something flashed red in the
trees surrounding the feeder, and I saw that the other parrots *were* there—well, two of them, at least. The yellow-eyed
bird was missing, but the other two just watched as the newcomer ate his stolen seed. I wondered if it was a betrayal of
some kind of bird code, letting the blue bird eat unaccosted
from the feeders while their obvious leader was away.

Scotty stepped out onto the deck, and the parrots disappeared in a flutter of wings and displaced branches. "You
ready for lunch, Grace?" he called across the lawn.

"Sure. Be right in!"

The back door closed and I hit Play on the video, using
my impending lunch break as an incentive to get through
five more minutes of footage. The video was from a gas station in Tacoma, a city just south of Seattle. I'd been surprised
when Scotty had sent it to me, but he just said that Marcus
knew what he was doing, and if he was looking in Tacoma,
there was a reason.

I'd already looked at the outdoor footage. It hadn't been

much help: cars pulled up to the pump; people got out, got their gas, and left. The gas station had seen better days. Its pavement was rutted with potholes, and two of the pumps had signs on them that must have meant they were out of order, because no one used them. Every now and then someone paid with a credit card and then punched angrily at the keypad before stalking toward the minimart that was part of the station. I figured receipts were hit-and-miss at the pump, which meant going inside to get one.

Now I was reviewing the indoor footage, which was trained outward from the register. I'd watched as a parade of customers had paid for gas, engaged in both angry and pleasant conversation with the small man behind the counter, bought packs of gum, Slim Jims, soda, Twinkies. It was funny the things you noticed without sound as a backdrop. More than one woman started to pay for her gas and then added a pack of Skittles or a packaged muffin, her posture guilty, sheepish, even on the security footage. People agonized over which lottery tickets to buy, sometimes leaving the store only to return a few minutes later for more, and lots of customers dug for exact change, seemingly oblivious to the person behind them, impatiently rolling their eyes.

I was getting ready to hit Pause again when an older man approached the register. He was balding, his hair entirely gone on top, a small fringe surrounding it like trees around a clearing. He had glasses, but they didn't seem to fit his face, and his nose looked a little too large for the rest of his features. He was wearing a stretched out T-shirt instead of the oversize suit, but I was sure it was the man from the used-car lot. He said something to the cashier, and the man pulled a carton of cigarettes from a rack behind him. While he pushed buttons on the register, the balding man reached up and touched the back of his head. For a split second, his scalp seemed to tilt, the hair ringing his bald spot slightly off center in the moment before he made another adjustment and set everything right.

It was a prosthetic. And maybe the nose, too.

I hit Pause and expanded the window, bringing the computer closer to my face.

But I already knew. I knew it from the determined set of the man's jaw, the arrogant line of his spine. He was trying to look down and out, like a lot of the people who stopped at the run-down little gas station. But he couldn't hide his sense of superiority. I felt it even through my computer, just like I'd felt it when I first saw him on the security footage from the used-car lot in Seattle. In spite of the lengths he'd gone to disguise himself, there was no doubt in my mind that my instincts had been right the first time.

It was Cormac.

Thirty-Five

I stood in the hallway later that night, listening to Scotty and Marcus talk about Seattle through their partially open bedroom door. At first they hadn't been sure it was Cormac, especially Marcus, who thought he would recognize Cormac even with an elaborate disguise. But Scotty had imported the picture to Photoshop, refined it, made it clearer. Then he'd sent it to a friend of his who did digital profiles for the LAPD. Scotty told the computer guy to make the nose smaller, give him hair like Cormac's, take off the glasses, dress him in a suit. When the picture came back a couple of hours later, there was no doubt in any of our minds that the guy who'd bought cigarettes at the crappy little minimart in Tacoma, Washington, was Cormac. He hadn't smoked when I'd lived with him, but I knew from experience that being on the run was its own special kind of hell. If anything would push someone back to a bad habit, that would be it.

"I wish I could stay," Scotty was saying, "but Wilson won't work with you. It's irregular even for him to work with me, but at least I was on the force here in LA. They'll let me stand on the sidelines as a courtesy. Besides, someone needs to stay with Grace."

"I don't have a problem staying with the kid. But I want to be there when they get him." Marcus sounded unusually agitated, but from the hallway I couldn't tell if it was annoyance or excitement in his voice. "I've waited a long time for this, Scott."

"I thought it wasn't about revenge? That it was about justice?" Scotty said. "If that's true, what does it matter if you're there?"

I heard Marcus's frustrated sigh. "Hell, I don't know. It just does."

There was a shuffling sound, a low murmur, and then Scotty's voice again. "They won't let you in on the bust anyway. You'd be stuck in some hotel around the corner, waiting for word from me. You'd hate it. Besides, there's no guarantee we'll even find him."

"Exactly." Marcus sounded a little desperate, even to me. "Which is why I should do the legwork while you team up with your pal Wilson."

"What about Grace?" Scotty asked.

I pushed their door open the rest of the way and stood in the doorway. "I'm coming too."

They turned to look at me. An open duffel bag, half filled

with neatly folded clothes, sat on the bed. Scotty had a bundle of socks in one hand.

He dropped the socks in the duffel and came toward me. "I understand why you'd want to be there, Grace, but you wouldn't be able to get close enough to see it go down anyway."

I folded my arms across my chest. "I don't care. I helped find him, and I want to be close by when you bring him in."

"Look, I get it," Marcus began, "believe me, I do. But if they don't want an old fogey like me there, you can bet your ass they're not signing off on a seventeen-year-old girl."

"They can't stop me from staying in a hotel around the corner." I looked at Marcus, sensing an opportunity to gain an ally. "And they can't stop you, either. Right, Scotty?"

Scotty sighed. "Not technically, no. But I think it would be better for both of you if you stayed here. I'll call you the minute something happens."

"But it's already been twelve days since he was at the used-car lot, and nine since he was in the minimart." The time-and-date stamps on the footage were burned in my memory. "We have to move fast, and you know the police aren't going to devote a lot of people to it. I mean, we don't know where he's staying or if he has a car. We don't even know which name he's using. Marcus and I can work on that stuff. We can go to the used-car lot and see if someone remembers him, can't we, Marcus?"

Marcus grinned a little. "You know it, kid."

Scotty folded his arms across his chest in an exact

imitation of my posture. "You're not going to give up, are you?"

I shook my head. "I can't. I need to do everything I can to get him. For Parker."

Scotty closed his eyes for a split second as his shoulders dropped. When he opened them again, I knew I'd won.

"You do everything I say," Scotty said. I knew it was no accident that he was looking at Marcus when he said it. "And I do mean everything. You might be Lord of the Grift, but I'm Prince of Police, and when we're on my turf, we play by my rules."

Marcus nodded a little too eagerly. "You got it."

Scotty turned his eyes on me. "And that goes double for you."

I held up my hands in a gesture of surrender. "You're the boss."

He walked to the closet and pulled down a tiny suitcase with wheels. "Be ready to leave in an hour."

Thirty-Six

It was dark by the time Marcus backed out of the driveway. I'd packed everything in the little suitcase Scotty had given me, including the new clothes, my books, and the pictures I'd taken with Scotty at the arcade. I didn't want to say anything to Scotty and Marcus, but I had no idea if I'd ever be back at the house on Colina Verde. Would the police take me into custody right after they got Cormac? Would I surrender in Seattle? Or come back to LA? I didn't know how any of it worked, and I'd closed the door on the guest room with a sharp pang of loss, wondering if I'd ever be safe inside its walls again.

The streets were dark as we headed for the freeway. We could have taken PCH to San Francisco, but that was the scenic route. We needed to get to Seattle and go to work as quickly as possible. I was already worried that Cormac might have moved on. If that was the case, we were really screwed, because I had no idea where he'd go next. I comforted myself with the knowledge that whatever happened, I was putting some distance between me and Detective Fletcher.

Scotty and Marcus argued over the radio. Scotty wanted an indie-rock station while Marcus fought for golden oldies that he pronounced "not so golden, but better than the junk that's on the rest of the radio." They settled on NPR, and we made our way north on the 405 to the sound of a British broadcaster interviewing a convict-turned-activist who was fighting to improve educational opportunities for inmates. I was comforted by the backseat of the Range Rover: the darkness, the buttery leather seats, the soft murmur of Scotty and Marcus talking about everything from the plantings in the front flower beds to a possible remodel on the upstairs bathroom. I looked out the window, taking in the streetlamps that threw orbs of light onto the asphalt, the homes and businesses of LA's suburbs twinkling like a galaxy all its own. I was glad to be leaving. I hoped everyone in Playa Hermosa was happy, that graduation would be all they dreamed it would be and that at least some of them would spend their last summer before college surfing and hanging at the Cove and going to Mike's together. But I didn't want to be there. It was too sharp a reminder of all I'd lost.

We left the city behind and everything went dark beyond the lights on the freeway. I thought of Parker, tried to imagine what he was doing, if he was safe and comfortable, if he missed me as much as I missed him. I thought about

Renee and her offer to start over. Was it that easy? Could I free Parker and simply join Renee, enroll in school, pretend that the last few months hadn't happened? I didn't know. I thought about Logan, too, getting ready for college and trying to take care of his mom. I didn't really believe in God, but I sent a little prayer out into the universe that they would be okay, that Warren would be home soon and Logan would go to college and they would be able to pretend the last few months hadn't happened too. Scotty would call it "sending light and love" to them. So I guess that's what I did: sent them light and love. Sometimes, I guess that's all you can do.

Somewhere along the way I must have dozed off, because I woke to a harsh blue light and the sound of something banging against the rear of the Range Rover. I sat up, my heart racing, and looked around.

We were at a gas station, and I was alone in the car. I turned in my seat and saw that Scotty was filling the SUV with gas. A couple of seconds later, Marcus emerged from the station's minimart with two bags in his hand. He opened the passenger side door and peered between the two front seats.

"Good, you're awake." He glanced at Scotty through the rearview window and passed me one of the bags. "The nutrition police have given us a road trip reprieve. Enjoy."

I looked inside the bag and found a Coke, a Snapple, two small bags of chips, a sad-looking apple (a gesture of appreciation for Scotty's leniency?), and a candy bar.

"Thanks," I said.

Marcus grinned. His thinning hair was messed up, and he almost looked a little crazy in the fluorescent light of the gas station. "No problem, kid. I bet we'll be able to get a diner breakfast out of him, too."

I laughed. "We can try." I opened the passenger side door. "I'm going to the bathroom while we're here."

When I returned, Scotty had finished getting gas and was in the driver's seat.

"Ready to go?" Scotty asked as I slid into the backseat.

"Yep."

We got back on the freeway and continued north. Scotty and Marcus entertained me with tales of their previous road trips, and I worked my way through the bag of snacks Marcus had given me. We switched off NPR and Scotty plugged his iPod into the car's dock. He agreed to let Marcus DJ if he promised to compromise, although Marcus's idea of "compromise" was different from everyone else's, so we ended up listening to an odd assortment of Frank Sinatra, Aretha Franklin, seventies folk music, and the occasional alternative hit insisted upon by Scotty. They sang along to some of it, and I pitched in when I knew the words. We were all singing "Three Little Birds" by Bob Marley, the sun just beginning to paint the sky a pale orange, when Scotty took the exit for Yreka, California.

"Let's grab breakfast and a room for a few hours," Scotty said, following the sign that indicated gas, food, and hotels to the left. "I'm beat."

I leaned forward in the backseat. "Are you sure we

shouldn't drive straight through?" I asked. "Marcus and I can help. That way we'll get there faster."

"But then we'll all be tired and out of sorts when we get there. No one sleeps well in a car." He turned into the parking lot for a Holiday Inn. "I know you're worried, but we'll get some food, sleep for a bit, and be back on the road before you know it."

I knew he was right, but I was itching to get to Seattle, terrified that Cormac would be gone when we got there. Where would Parker be then? I thought about Renee. Would I be willing to entrap her if we couldn't find Cormac? Pretend to take her up on her offer and then hand her over to the police? I wasn't sure, and I didn't want to think too hard about why I hadn't considered it already. Could I really still care about her? Feel connected to her in spite of all she'd done? If so, I was more screwed up than I thought.

The hotel lobby was like that of any other midlevel hotel: the smell of coffee and carpet, generic artwork, and potted plants strategically placed in the corners. Marcus reserved adjoining rooms from a sleepy-looking girl who probably wasn't much older than me, and we went upstairs to drop our bags before heading to the attached café for breakfast.

Marcus took full advantage of the opportunity to order all the greasy food he could find on the menu. He dug into a sausage and cheese omelet with gusto while Scotty, a bowl of oatmeal and fresh fruit in front of him, looked on with a mixture of shock and disapproval. When we were done, we went back to the hotel. I closed the door that connected our rooms and took a hot shower, got into my pajamas, and climbed into bed. Scotty had been right: it was a lot nicer than curling up in the backseat, and I was more tired than I'd realized.

Still, I couldn't sleep. I thought about Parker and Logan, wondering what they were doing, if they were okay out there, battling their respective demons, both in some way because of me.

The room suddenly seemed smaller, like the walls were gradually closing in on me. Maybe it was the taupe paint, the framed desert scenes on the walls, the wheeze of the air conditioner near the window, but I was suddenly back at the Motel 6, scared and alone when I first came back to California.

I sat up and slid out of bed, padding across the room on bare feet. I hesitated at the door that connected my room to Marcus and Scotty's room, then knocked.

"Come in." Scotty's voice came from the other side of the door. I opened it hesitantly and peered into the room. He was propped up on one arm, the bedside lamp on, Marcus snoring softly beside him. "Is everything all right?"

"I . . . I'm not sure," I said, feeling stupid. "I felt . . . I was a little scared. I don't know why."

"Are you okay now?" he asked. "Can I get you anything?"

I shook my head. "I think I'm better now."

"Do you want to leave the door open?"

"Are you sure it's okay?" I asked.

"Of course," he said. "Marcus is out anyway, and I can barely keep my eyes open."

I nodded. "Maybe I will. Thanks."

I walked quietly back to my room and got into bed, keeping my eyes on the faint wash of light coming from the open door between our rooms. A few minutes later, I heard Scotty's voice.

"Sweet dreams, Grace."

"Sweet dreams," I said.

I turned out the light and was asleep almost instantly.

Thirty-Seven

We got to Tacoma about six that night. It was nothing like Bellevue. Bellevue was urban chic: organic food markets, expensive bistros, and high-end retailers, all of it frequented by rich people who liked to pretend they were just like everyone else. A little seedy and run down, Tacoma was Bellevue's ugly older sister. It was easy to picture the little gas station where I'd spotted Cormac on one of the pitted streets lined with sad minimalls and fast-food places.

Scotty checked us in to a Best Western near the stadium and immediately left to meet his contact at the Tacoma PD. While he was gone, Marcus and I unpacked and went to a nearby diner for food. We were back in Marcus and Scotty's room watching an old episode of 24 when Scotty finally returned. He didn't have much to tell us. He was going to meet Detective Wilson Ling, an old colleague from the

LAPD, at the station the next day and see what kind of resources they could drum up from inside the department. In the meantime, Marcus and I would visit the used-car lot and look into the surrounding area. We'd brought pictures of Cormac—both the one in disguise and the one that had been Photoshopped by Scotty's friend—to show hotels and restaurants in the area. It was the only thing we could do with the information we had, and I was all too aware of how little it was, how thin the string on which Parker's freedom hung.

I took a shower and got into bed. I was reading when a knock sounded from the door between our rooms.

"Come in."

Scotty poked his head into my room. "Mind if I leave this open a crack tonight? I'm probably just being paranoid, but I'd feel better."

I smiled. He was trying to make it seem like he wanted the door open for his own peace of mind, when really, he was trying to make me feel less alone. "Sure."

"Great. Sleep well, honey."

"You too."

I read a little bit longer, the sound of Scotty and Marcus's softly spoken conversation in the other room a soothing backdrop to the hum of the room's air conditioner. When I turned out the light, I had no trouble falling asleep.

Detective Ling picked up Scotty early the next morning, and Marcus and I took the Range Rover to the used-car lot. I was more than a little surprised by the tiny, run-down lot lined with cars. Without the context of everything around it, the security camera had made the place look big, but really it was no bigger than the small parking lot above the Cove.

Marcus parked the car in one of two open spots near a stucco building with dirty windows. He leaned forward, gazing at the office through the windshield of the Range Rover. "Tough times, eh, Cormac?" he said under his breath.

There was no malice in it, just a kind of casual resignation, like Cormac was right there beside him. I was suddenly nervous. I'd gotten comfortable with Marcus and Scotty, but I was on the run, too.

"Can't we just break in later tonight and look at the sales records?" I asked. "It doesn't look like there's any security, and we already know where the camera is."

Marcus shook his head. "Won't work. If Cormac did buy a car here, he did it under the table. I doubt he's had the money for a good ID, and certainly not one that will pass muster with the government. He can't exactly waltz into the DMV and register a new vehicle."

I sighed. "Okay, then."

Marcus turned to me. "You okay?" I nodded, and he opened his car door. "Let's go, kid."

We got out of the car and went inside. Immediately a pot-bellied man with skinny legs approached us with a smile. His eyes crinkled at the corners, and his hair was thick and a little too brown. After all my running, I knew hair dye, and I pegged the guy for someone who was covering his gray with cheap bottles of drugstore color.

"Morning!" he said. "Nice day to buy a new car!"

"Morning," Marcus said. "I suppose so."

He sounded different, minus the ever-present sarcasm and at-everyone-else's-expense humor that I'd come to love. He was in work mode, his expression earnest as he looked out the window, surveying the lineup of old cars.

The man extended his hand and Marcus shook it. "I'm Ron Lysinsky," the guy said. "What can I do you for?" He laughed a little at his joke.

Marcus clasped the man on his back. I almost felt sorry for him. He looked so happy that Marcus was friendly, like Marcus was a guaranteed sale, but I knew it was a gesture meant to establish subtle dominance.

"I'm hoping you can help me out," Marcus said conspiratorially. "You see, I'm looking for a friend of mine. Thought he said he'd meet us at the Travelodge, but he never showed. Now I'm thinking I got it wrong, but I lost my damn cell phone on the ferry. You know how it is. Goddamn technology. Can't live with it, can't live without it."

Ron shrank a little under Marcus's hand, his demeanor becoming more guarded, even a little pissed off with the news that we weren't there to buy a car after all.

"I don't know how I can help you," he said, stepping away from Marcus's hand. It was an evolutionary reflex, survival instinct: try to get out from under the hand—figurative or literal—that held you in submission.

"Thing is," Marcus said, "he mentioned buying a car here. I'm hoping you can point me in the right direction with an address or something."

Ron shook his head. "Can't do that. It would be a violation of our customers' privacy."

Marcus nodded, like he was considering the argument. After a few seconds he took ahold of Ron's arm. "Ron—can I call you Ron?" The guy barely had time to nod. Marcus cast a quick glance at me and continued talking. "Can I talk to you in private for a second?"

But Marcus was already leading him to the wall that separated a glass-fronted office from the rest of the space. I watched as he lowered his head toward Ron's very brown hair, murmuring in low, soothing tones. I didn't mind that I was left out of the negotiation. I just wanted to find Cormac. I didn't care how we did it.

The two went back and forth for a couple of minutes. At one point, Ron glanced up at me before turning his gaze to the concrete floor under his loafers. Marcus said something else, and then Ron was talking, speaking in an anguished almost whisper that told me he wasn't happy about the information he was giving up. Marcus shook his hand, and less than ten minutes after we walked into the place, we were on our way back out to the Range Rover, Marcus's hand draped protectively around my shoulder.

"Did you get anything?" I asked when we were back inside the car.

Marcus glanced over, a look of surprise on his face. "Did you think I wouldn't?"

"I don't know," I said. "I wasn't sure. What did you tell him?"

Marcus started the car and reversed out of the parking space. "I told him your dad had run out on you, that I was your uncle and was trying to catch up with my bastard of a brother to make him do right by his kid."

"Wow . . . good one," I said, thinking it wasn't far from the truth. "So what did he say?"

Marcus turned onto the main road and headed back for the hotel. "He said the guy in the picture came in about two weeks ago, wanted to buy a car under the table, no records."

"And?"

"And Ron said no, which proves that he's smarter than he looks. Selling a car without officially transferring title and registration is a good way to get yourself locked up."

"So we didn't get anything." I heard the defeat in my voice.

Marcus grinned. "I didn't say that."

"Then what? You're killing me," I said.

"Ron said the guy was nervous, tried to make small talk before he approached the idea of a car, mentioned that he was staying in a motel in the area."

I waited for him to say more. He didn't. "That's it? That's our lead? 'A motel in the area'?" I took a deep breath, realizing that I sounded a little hysterical.

"It's not much," Marcus admitted, "but look on the plus side: Cormac probably hasn't been able to get out of town without a car. And he walked into that gas station to buy cigarettes, so I'm betting he's somewhere in close proximity to it."

"Did the used-car guy—"

"Ron," Marcus corrected.

I sighed. "Did Ron know Cormac's name—the name he's using right now?"

"No, but that's okay. If everything else is any indication, Cormac's staying in some shithole near that gas station. Shitholes don't have a lot of rooms. We'll work outward from the station, start watching them for people coming and going."

I thought about it. "What about the gas station itself?"

"What about it?" Marcus asked.

"Maybe one of us should watch it, just in case it's his regular cigarette-buying place, while the other one checks out the motels."

Marcus raised his eyebrows. "His regular cigarette-buying place? Is that a technical term?"

I rolled my eyes. "You know what I mean."

He nodded. "It's a good idea." We stopped at a red light and he looked over at me. "You know, kid, you're not half bad at this. Not that I recommend it for you going forward."

Thirty-Eight

Scotty's news was better than ours. Thanks to Detective Ling, an APB had been put out on Cormac in the Seattle-Tacoma area. We were back in the hotel, debriefing, when Scotty handed me the sheet of paper.

There were two pictures of Cormac: one with the disguise he'd used at the gas station and used-car lot, and the one that Scotty's friend in LA had doctored to look more like the Cormac I remembered. But what really surprised me was the name—or names—underneath the photograph.

WANTED AS A PERSON OF INTEREST IN GRAND THEFT:
PETER BUKOWSKI
aka PETER AIKEN
aka CORMAC AIKEN
aka CORMAC LITHGOW

aka CORMAC McBRIDE

aka CORMAC NEIL

aka CORMAC SINCLAIR

aka CORMAC ROLLINS

aka CORMAC FONTAINE

I'd known Cormac had other aliases. I just didn't realize how many.

"Where did these come from?" I asked.

"Some of them came from you," Scotty said. "The rest came from Marcus."

"And I'm sure there are more," Marcus said. "There was a good ten years between the time he ditched me and found Renee and then adopted you and Parker. He wasn't watching *Oprah* and eating bonbons all that time."

I handed Scotty back the piece of paper. "So what now?"

"I'm going to work with Detective Ling tomorrow. The TPD won't give us anybody else, but the chief agreed to let Wilson and me run down some other car lots in the area, see if Cormac tried to buy something from someone else. It's the best I can do given that I told the department my interest in the case is personal."

"That's great," I said. "With you and Detective Ling on that angle and Marcus and me on the motels and the gas station, we'll make good time."

"Why don't you let Wilson and me take the motels and the gas station?" Scotty asked it like a question, but I had the feeling it was more of a statement. "I'm sure once we hit the used-car lots tomorrow I can get some more time out of the department to case the other places."

"No way," I said. "I'm not sitting here watching TV and ordering room service while you're out looking for Cormac. Besides, it'll be faster if we split up."

"Kid's right," Marcus said. "Cormac could leave any second. We can't afford to wait around and see if the TPD will give you the go-ahead to question motel managers or case the gas station. Grace and I are here. Let us do it."

Scotty rubbed his chin. "I don't like Grace being in the line of fire."

"What line of fire?" I asked, desperate to make my point. Parker's trial date was less than two weeks away. The window to help him was closing. "There's no line of fire. I'll be out of the way, an observer."

"I don't want Grace in danger any more than you do," Marcus said to Scotty, "but I can put her across from the gas station while I check out the motels. We'll be within blocks of each other. If Grace spots Cormac, all she has to do is text me and I'll be there."

"It's not like I'd confront him on my own," I said. "Please, Scotty . . . we're running out of time."

Scotty sighed. "We'll try it out tomorrow." He met my eyes, his voice turning stern. "But Grace, I'm not kidding about this: You stay out of sight. If you even think you see him, you text Marcus or me, got it?"

"I promise."

Scotty nodded, but he didn't look happy about the idea.

An hour later we were at dinner when my cell phone rang. The number was blocked, which meant it could only be one person.

"I have to take this," I said to Scotty and Marcus. "I'll be right back."

I slid out of the booth and walked to the front of the restaurant, then pressed the button to accept the call. "Hey."

"Hey, Gracie," Renee said on the other end of the phone.

I cringed at the nickname but didn't correct her. "Hey. What's up?"

"Just checking on you," she said. "Have you thought about everything? About what I said?"

I kicked my foot against the side of the restaurant, leaving black scuff marks on the toe of my tennis shoes. "I can't."

I hadn't been aware of making the decision, but as soon as I said it, I knew it was the right one. Too much had changed. I had changed. Renee and I might be able to build something new, but we'd only be tacking something pretty on top of an already-fractured foundation. Nothing we built together would ever be solid.

"Grace . . ." She spoke softly, her voice full of sadness. "What else will you do? Where else will you go?"

I swallowed against the fear that rose in my throat. "I don't know." And I didn't. I only knew that the way forward wasn't reliving the mistakes from my past. I'd have to take a chance on a fresh start, have some faith that whatever the path ahead, moving forward was better than trying to go back.

"Are you sure?" she asked. "Because I might not be able to risk surfacing again."

I hesitated. We were close to Cormac. I could feel it. If we lost him, there wouldn't be time to create a sting to bring in Renee before Parker's trial date. That's what I told myself, anyway, all the while avoiding what I suspected was the real reason: in some secret part of my twisted brain I still cared about Renee. All that mother-daughter bonding time might have been fake, but I hadn't known it at the time, and it had left its mark on me whether I liked it or not.

"I know."

She didn't say anything for so long that I was beginning to think we'd been disconnected when she finally spoke again. "I'll . . . Well, I'll miss you, Gracie."

I thought her voice sounded thick and heavy, and I wondered if she could be crying. I'd never seen her cry. Not once in all the years I'd known her. I wanted to say it back, to tell her I'd miss her too, but only because that was what people said in this kind of situation. The truth was, I'd miss what I'd thought she was, what I'd thought we were together. I didn't know her well enough to miss the real her.

"Good-bye, Renee." I said the words softly into the phone and hung up. Then I leaned against the restaurant, trying to get used to the idea that I would never see her again.

Thirty-Nine

Detective Ling picked Scotty up before breakfast the next day. Marcus and I drove down to the waterfront and ate muffins on a bench near the water. When we were done, I opened my phone to call Detective Castillo in Playa Hermosa.

"Keep it short," Marcus instructed as I dialed.

I nodded. I'd practiced what I wanted to say in my head. It was less than a minute. Allowing for some response from Castillo, I'd still be off the phone in under two minutes, and Marcus and I would leave right afterward.

"Hello?"

"It's Grace."

"Grace . . ." He exhaled into the phone and I wondered if it was the sound of relief or annoyance. "It's been a while."

"I know," I said. "I'm getting close to that thing we talked about, and I need to know if you'll still vouch for

Parker and me if I can make it happen."

"Well, you know I can't guarantee anything, but I think you have a good shot." He paused. "Where are you? Maybe I can round up resources, come help you out."

"No, thanks," I said. "I'm doing it my way. I just need to know if you'll be there when I call with the news . . . if you'll be there when it's time to help Parker and me."

"I'll be there, Grace." His voice was firm. "You have my word."

I nodded, even though I knew he couldn't see it. "Good. I'll call you back soon."

I disconnected the call and looked at the timer on my phone. One minute twenty-nine seconds.

"Good job," Marcus said. "Now let's get out of here."

He dropped me at El Tapatio, the little Mexican food place across the street from the gas station where I'd spotted Cormac.

"I'll be within a two-mile radius. Text if you see him. Text if you even think you see him." He seemed to hesitate.

"I will, I promise." I hurried inside before he could change his mind about leaving me there.

The restaurant was a tiny hole-in-the-wall with linoleum floor and Formica tables. I ordered a soda from a beautiful brown-skinned girl with a perfect smile and curly brown hair. She reminded me of Selena, and I suddenly regretted not saying good-bye to her. I wondered if I'd see her again before she went to Nicaragua. We were operating in different spheres now, two planets orbiting different suns.

I took my soda to a booth against the front window. It gave me a perfect view of the gas station. It looked even worse in person: small and dirty and neglected. I opened my book for show, trained my eyes on the building across the street, and settled in to wait.

The station didn't get a lot of customers. A trickle of cars stopped for gas, a few of the people going inside for one reason or another. More than one person entered the minimart on foot. They emerged shaking packs of cigarettes against their hands or carrying gallons of milk or a handful of lottery tickets. It was after one in the afternoon when Marcus called.

"Hey, kid. How you holding up?"

"Nothing's happening here," I said. "How about you?"

"These places are ghost towns," he said.

I sighed. "Well, it's only the first day."

"Don't tell me; you're a glass-half-full kind of girl?" he said wryly.

I laughed. "Not usually." Maybe Scotty was rubbing off on me. It definitely wasn't Marcus's influence.

"Call if you need me." He hung up before I could respond.

The girl at the counter was starting to glance suspiciously my way, so I ordered two tacos and another soda and made small talk while she put my lunch together. I told her I was on a business trip with my dad and needed a place to escape the hotel, someplace quiet where I could read without my dad asking me a million questions. It was thin, but she laughed and seemed to understand.

I took my food back to the table by the window and pretended to read, but by the time Marcus pulled up in the Range Rover at four thirty in the afternoon, I still hadn't seen any sign of Cormac.

"This sucks," I said as I climbed into the front seat.

"Totally blows," he agreed.

I laughed at his terminology and he drove us back to the hotel. Scotty hadn't made progress either. None of the used-car lots in the area had recognized Cormac's pictures, and we assumed that he'd given up after trying to buy an under-the-table car from Ron Lysinsky.

We were all quiet at dinner, and I was relieved to fall into the hotel bed at the end of the night. I turned out the light and grabbed my phone from where it was charging on the nightstand. Pulling up the calendar, I counted the days until June twenty-ninth. There were only twelve of them. Twelve days standing between Parker and prison.

Forty

The days morphed together in a loop of continental breakfasts, conversation with Marisa (the counter girl and cook
at El Tapatio), and hour upon hour staring at the tiny gas
station. Wilson Ling's chief had granted Ling permission to
continue working with Scotty, and they had been running
down the few leads that trickled in from the APB, supposed
sightings of Cormac that never came to anything solid. In
between, Scotty worked the Seattle and Tacoma police data-
bases, looking through lists of parking tickets and moving
violations (both were long shots if Cormac didn't have a car,
but we were getting desperate), drunk-and-disorderlies,
anything that might lead us to Cormac.

Marcus was slowly crossing motels off his list. His MO
was simple: take Cormac's picture to the hotel manager, ask
if he or she had seen the man in the photograph, then case

the place for a couple of days in case the manager was lying or mistaken.

In the meantime, I worked the gas station. I'd had one false alarm—a man who stopped for gas looked enough like Cormac that I actually texted Marcus—but he was just a middle-aged guy in a baggy suit.

Cormac hadn't surfaced.

"Hola, Sarah!" Marisa called out when I entered El Tapatio a week after we'd started our stakeout.

I'd told her my parents were divorced and I was forced to spend the summer with my dad. I tried to keep the details fuzzy—our estranged relationship, my dad's obsessive attention to work, the necessity of following him to conferences in crappy towns all over the United States during our summers together—to avoid lying more than I had to. But I still felt shitty. I *was* lying. It was something I'd hoped not to do anymore, and I had to remind myself that the lies weren't designed to hurt anyone or steal from anyone, that they were just to free Parker, who didn't deserve what had happened to him. But it didn't really help. I wanted out of this kind of life, and sometimes it felt like I would never be free of it. Like it had its claws in me so deep, the only thing I could do was keep moving forward, dragging it behind me like an animal trap clamped to my leg. Sometimes I even wished for my former obliviousness, for the days when I was so naive, so entrenched in Cormac and Renee's propaganda, that I could rationalize anything. But that Grace was gone forever, and as Marcus would say, the new one didn't blow sunshine up my ass.

"*Hola!* Did you watch the next episode of *Buffy* last night?" I'd been watching the show with Marcus when Scotty was busy with Detective Ling in the evenings and had managed to convince Marisa to give it a try.

She shook her head and poured my soda. "I had too much work around the house. Did you?"

I nodded.

"Don't tell me!" she said before I could say anything.

I laughed and pressed my lips together. We talked for a few more minutes and I took the soda to my seat near the window. I grimaced as I sat down. My capris had gotten a little tight in the past few weeks—too many good Scotty meals in Playa Hermosa, continental breakfasts with Marcus, tacos and enchiladas made by Marisa. I'd needed to gain the weight, but now I was uncomfortable, and I didn't dare say anything to Scotty, who would force me to go clothes shopping and leave the gas station unattended.

I looked at the calendar on my phone and was surprised to realize that it was June twenty-fifth. I'd known there were only four days to the start of Parker's trial, but I hadn't been keeping track of the actual date; tonight, the fate of Playa Hermosa's peacocks would be determined by the town's residents. I hoped they'd be allowed to stay.

I opened my book and looked across the street. The cloudy sky cast everything in shades of gray, but at least it wasn't raining. I'd spent a couple of tough days peering out at the gas station through the rain-streaked window of El

Tapatio before I'd become desperate and gone outside. The first time, I'd gotten drenched leaning against the building. I got smarter after that and had started tucking a pocket umbrella into my bag, just in case. Still, rain wasn't ideal for the work I was doing, and I hoped the stormy sky wasn't a portent of worse things to come.

The gas station was business as usual. The place would have looked deserted if not for a woman filling her older-model Toyota Corolla at one of the pumps. I took a drink of my soda as I scanned the surrounding area. A few seconds later, a teenager wearing baggy cargo shorts and a shapeless polo shirt came into view. It wasn't until he came closer that I realized he wasn't a teenager, but a grown man.

He was wearing a bucket hat not unlike the ones Marcus wore when he was out in the sun, but it was still obvious that the guy was bald or almost bald, and I could see glasses perched on his nose under the brim of the hat. But his shoulders hung a little too low for the man to be Cormac. He didn't walk with Cormac's purpose, with the right blend of arrogance and dynamism that somehow made people both revere and like the man I had thought of as my father.

I watched him anyway. Parker's swiftly approaching trial date and my own frustration were making me desperate. I was seeing things where they didn't exist, as if my wanting something to be true could alter the course of the universe, conjure progress out of thin air. The man was almost to the gas station, his body angled slightly toward it, away from my vantage point, as he aimed for the minimart. I watched as he approached the door and disappeared inside.

I took another drink of my soda. A couple of minutes later, the man emerged, carrying a carton of cigarettes. I strained to get a look at the box tucked under his arm. He shifted a little as the door closed behind him, stepping out of the way as the woman with the Corolla reached for it, and then I saw the carton more clearly. The black-and-white footage on the security camera made it impossible to match the colors, but the font on the box was the same, tall and a little blocky.

Marlboro. The same brand purchased by Cormac on the original footage from the gas station.

Leaning forward in my seat, I kept my eyes on his face, shadowed under the brim of the hat. He stopped and opened the carton of cigarettes, withdrawing one of the packs and shaking it against the palm of his hand. A moment later he bent to the trash can to throw the wrapping away. His hat slid off his head, falling to the pavement at his feet and revealing the top of a nearly bald head. He squatted down to retrieve the hat, then stood, reaching a hand up to scratch the top of his scalp.

Cormac's voice echoed through my memory: *These things itch like a son of a bitch.*

He'd spoken the words during some long-ago con, scratching his head while he'd been wearing a silver wig. In any other situation, it might have been a coincidence, but now I saw it—the familiar set of his mouth, the lines, now deeper, around his eyes.

It was him. It was Cormac.

I spent an indeterminate time just staring at him, debating whether I could be wrong. Then he was on the move, heading back the way he'd come. It mobilized me, and I jumped up, nearly spilling my soda, and headed for the door.

"See you later, Sarah?" Marisa called after me.

I didn't have time to answer. I was out the door and crossing the street. I was tailing him when I realized I hadn't called Marcus or Scotty. Afraid to alert Cormac to my presence, I turned off my ringer and dialed Scotty's number, then slipped my phone back into my pocket. He had been a cop. I hoped he'd get the idea.

Cormac walked to the end of the next block and turned right at an abandoned factory building. Still moving, he bent his head, and a moment later the smell of tobacco drifted in his wake. I was gaining on him, too worried about losing sight of him to even think about what I'd do once I caught up. My heart pounded harder and faster as we got farther away from the main road. If I lost him now, I might never see him again, and prison time for Parker would be all but guaranteed.

We made a left and crossed the street to another block lined with crumbling Victorians that may or may not have been occupied. Across the street was a vacant lot, the grass dead and knee-high. I had no weapons, nothing to defend myself with, and no way to keep Cormac here until help arrived. All I could do was keep my eyes on him.

There was only twenty feet between us when his footsteps started to slow. By the time he stopped walking, we were less than ten feet apart. I stopped when he did, waiting to see what he'd do next, getting ready to run, hoping Scotty was on his way. We were only a couple of blocks from the gas station, and the neighborhood was almost entirely deserted. It wouldn't take Scotty long to find me if he started at the station.

The man in front of me turned slowly around, the carton of cigarettes still in his hand. And then we were face-to-face.

"Grace." He didn't even look surprised.

"Cormac." I wondered if Scotty was listening, if he knew where I was.

The prosthetics confused my already-freaked-out brain. It was both Cormac and not Cormac. There was Cormac's mouth, Cormac's eyes, Cormac's hands. But his features were twisted, his nose bulbous, his eyes big and watery behind the thick glasses.

"How did you find me?" he finally asked.

"Does it matter?" And then, because I needed to keep him talking: "You promised to go back for Parker."

Every nerve in my body was coiled like a viper. When he dropped his cigarette butt to the ground and reached for his pocket, I jumped a little, prepared for him to take off. Instead he pulled out the pack of cigarettes he'd opened at the gas station and lit another.

"I wasn't in a position to go back for Parker," he said. "We were still getting set up with Miranda."

"Miranda. Another victim," I said bitterly.

His eyes hardened. "People make themselves victims, Grace. You should know that by now."

I swallowed the complex storm of emotion that rose in my chest. "I don't buy your bullshit anymore, Cormac. Nobody asks to be made a victim. Trusting people and being nice and believing that people are good . . . that's not the problem. We were. You are. All of those people we hurt and lied to and stole from? They didn't deserve what happened to them. That's just a bedtime story you tell yourself. Only you've been telling it for so long you actually believe it."

He took a drag on the cigarette. "And what about you, Gracie? What bedtime stories do you tell yourself?"

"I don't," I say. "I'm not doing that anymore."

He shrugged. "So what now? Why'd you come back?" He looked around, like he expected someone to be with me. "You think you can convince me to turn myself in? Cut a deal for Parker?" He laughed a little. "You would have had better luck if you hadn't stolen my money, forced me out of the game with Miranda."

"I already know you won't turn yourself in." I heard the sadness in my voice and wondered how I still had the capacity to be sad about Cormac and Renee. I guess sadness wasn't some kind of reservoir you could drain dry. It was more like an underground spring, always replenished through some secret source hidden under the surface.

"Then what's the point? Closure?" he asked.

I shifted on my feet. How long had we been standing

here? Had my phone dialed Scotty? Had the call dropped? Was he on his way?

"I came to get you," I said. It was the truth, but it was lame. I hadn't been able to do anything on my own. I sure as hell wasn't going to bring Cormac in.

"Sorry to disappoint you, Grace. But I have things to do. Take care."

He turned to walk away, and for a few seconds all I could do was watch him go, my former rage impotent and silent. Then something small but persistent started to scream in the recesses of my mind. It rattled the bars of its cage, determined to get my attention.

I ran forward so fast that he didn't even start to turn around until I was almost on him. When he did, I grabbed his arm and started pulling and screaming. I didn't know where I was taking him, didn't even know what I was saying, but I tugged at his arm, trying to drag him back toward the gas station like I could bring him in myself.

He was stronger than I expected. His free hand clamped down painfully on the arm that was holding him. I cried out, but I held on. If I let him go, it was over.

He grunted, prying at my fingers, trying to remove them, but I held fast, digging my short nails into the flesh of his forearm. For a second, I thought I had him. I didn't know what I would do with him, but it seemed that he couldn't shake me, and I felt a moment's triumph right before the back of his free hand connected like a brick to the side of my face.

I fell back onto the pavement and was still trying to register what had happened when he started running. I watched him get smaller, my vision blurry and out of focus.

He'd almost reached the corner when a car came into view at the end of the street. But it wasn't a police car, and I dropped my head back to the pavement and watched Cormac slow down as the front door of the car opened. Two figures emerged. Someone was coming for Cormac. He had new partners now, and they were coming to help him. I'd never see him again, and I'd probably never see Parker again either. I'd been stupid. Stupid to think I could catch Cormac and stupid to let Renee go. Hope leaked from my body as I struggled to sit up, commanded my brain to obey.

And then someone spoke. No, not spoke. Shouted.

"Stop! Police! Put your hands up!"

Two blurry objects came into view at the end of the block, stopping next to the first car. My vision got fuzzier as the movement on the street increased. And then Scotty's face was above me, his eyes dark and worried, his hands gentle on my forehead.

"It's okay, honey. Just hang on. Everything's going to be okay."

Forty-One

I shifted in my seat at the front of the courtroom. Scotty and Marcus were next to Detective Castillo in the row behind me, and Logan and his mother were at the back of the room. Detective Fletcher hadn't come. I guess he was looking for his next piece of steak. Selena wasn't there, either. She had texted me from the airport, on her way to Nicaragua, after we got back from Seattle.

It didn't matter. Everyone else was in the periphery. My eyes were on the doors at the side of the room.

"You ready?" a voice whispered.

I turned to face the woman next to me. Her name was Kate Levy, and she had copper-colored hair and kind green eyes. Scotty and Marcus had insisted on hiring her to represent Parker and me. They'd waved me away when I promised to pay them back.

I nodded, trying to swallow the nervousness that seemed to block my airway.

She met my eyes. "Just remember what I said: Keep your answers short and sweet. Don't volunteer anything. The plea has been arranged, so this is just a formality." She smiled. "Everything will be fine."

I wanted to smile at her, but I was starting to feel sick to my stomach. The pessimism that had kept me alive all my life was fighting against my fledgling belief that when you did the right thing, everything would somehow be okay. There would always be tough things, hard things, but there would be good things, too. It was one of Scotty's many New Agey beliefs that made sense to me, and I'd vowed to do my part from here on out, to do the right thing and let the chips fall where they may. That was one of Marcus's sayings, but I'd found that Marcus's peculiar brand of wisdom came in handy just as often as Scotty's, the two of them a perfect mix of practicality and faith.

I glanced at the table on the opposite side of the courtroom. The plea had been orchestrated by Kate, but I recognized the assistant DA—his name was Brandon Melville—from the news. A woman stood next to him in a crisp pencil skirt and suit, but I had no idea who she was.

Detective Ling had called Detective Castillo as soon as they had Cormac in custody. It had taken over a week—and an official delay in Parker's trial date—to extradite Cormac to Playa Hermosa. I'd given them a new description of Renee along with my cell phone. Maybe their tech geniuses would be able to do something to track it. I was still confused about my feelings for her, but I couldn't afford to feel bad. We'd all paid a price for what we did—Logan and his family most of all. It wouldn't be fair to protect her. I'd been afraid that Scotty and Marcus would be mad that I'd kept my meeting with Renee from them, but Scotty had just draped an arm over my shoulders and squeezed, and Marcus hadn't said a word. Somehow I think they understood. After that, the details of the plea had been handled by Kate and the DA's office until they'd reached an agreement that Kate said was fair.

Everyone swiveled as the door opened at the side of the courtroom. A uniformed bailiff stepped through the doorway, and behind him, another bailiff holding on to Parker's arm.

I stood, forcing myself to remain in place. I hadn't seen him since the night he'd dropped me off at Logan's house almost seven months before. The night we'd stolen the Fairchilds' gold. He was thinner, his body lost in the folds of the suit Kate had sent for him to wear to court. He also looked older, the hard angles of his face accentuated by the short haircut he now wore.

But he was still Parker, and his eyes scanned the courtroom until they found mine. When they did, I couldn't keep the smile from my face. The corners of his mouth turned up just a little as the bailiffs escorted him to the defendants' table and the chair next to mine.

"Grace . . ." He breathed my name, like he couldn't believe

it was me. He shook his head. "How did you do it?"

I smiled. "I had help."

I turned and introduced him to Scotty and Marcus, and I could see that they were sizing Parker up like protective parents, trying to connect the dots, to match all the things I'd told them about Parker with the person who stood in front of them.

"Thank you," Parker said to them. "For everything you've done for Grace. And for me."

A sharp voice barked from the front of the courtroom before they could respond.

"All rise for the honorable Judge Elizabeth Hancock."

We faced the front of the courtroom and watched as a woman in a long black robe stepped up to the judge's seat.

"Please be seated," Judge Hancock said. "Now calling for the record the case of the people of the State of California versus Parker Dawson, and, concurrently, the people of the State of California versus Grace Abbott. Counsel, please identify yourself for the record."

"Kate Levy for the defendants Ms. Abbott and Mr. Dawson, Your Honor."

Judge Hancock turned her eyes on the other table.

"Brandon Melville, representing the County of Los Angeles, Your Honor." The woman next to him spoke next. "Maude Gillcrest, family court social worker, Your Honor."

"Thank you," Judge Hancock said. She looked at Kate Levy. "Has counsel advised the defendants against concurrent proceedings?"

Kate nodded. "I have, Your Honor. However, since a plea agreement has been reached with Mr. Melville's office, the defendants have opted to stand together."

Judge Hancock nodded, dropping her gaze to a stack of papers in front of her. She paged through them for a few seconds before speaking again. "I see a plea has been reached in exchange for your cooperation in the apprehension of Peter Bukowski. Terms and conditions as follows: For Parker Dawson, a reduced charge of ten counts misdemeanor vandalism, one count accessory to petty theft. Sentence will be five years' probation, one hundred hours' community service, and time served. Should Mr. Dawson commit further crimes during his five-year probationary period, he will be immediately remanded back to Los Angeles County Jail." She leveled her gaze at Parker. "Do you accept this plea, Mr. Dawson?"

"Yes, Your Honor," Parker said.

"Very well." The judge turned her eyes on me. "For Grace Abbott, a reduced charge of trespassing, one count petty theft, one count felony fraud. Sentence will be five years' probation and one hundred hours' community service. Furthermore, the minor defendant will remain in the custody of Mr. Scott Thompson and Mr. Marcus Fitzgerald until this Friday, after which time she will be remanded into the custody of Child Protective Services until her eighteenth birthday, effective . . ." She looked down, checking her calendar. "Next February twentieth. Do you accept the terms and conditions of this plea, Ms. Abbott?"

I hesitated. Not because I didn't want the deal. The alternative was jail, and I definitely didn't want that. But I'd avoided thinking about leaving Scotty and Marcus. Now it was right in front of me, only four days away. I'd be back in foster care, back to living with people I didn't know, being wary, hoping for the best. But it was part of my new plan: finish high school, go to college, build a life that no one could take away from me. Scotty and Marcus had promised to keep in touch wherever I was, and I'd be eighteen in just seven months. This was what it meant to make good choices—doing the right thing even when it was hard.

"Ms. Abbott?" Judge Hancock said again. "Do you accept the terms and conditions of this plea?"

"Yes, Your Honor."

She nodded. "Very well."

After that, everything moved quickly. Judge Hancock repeated the details of our plea agreements and Parker and I repeated our acceptance of them under oath. We had to answer a bunch of questions: were we under any kind of duress in our acceptance of the plea, were we under the influence of drugs or alcohol, did we know we were entitled to a trial if we wanted one. About twenty minutes later, Judge Hancock instructed us to contact the Office of Probation. Then it was over, and I had a few seconds to hug Parker before they took him away to sign the papers that would set him free.

Kate Levy shook my hand. "Good luck, Ms. Abbott. I hope you get the second chance you deserve."

"Thank you." I found myself choking back tears, not because it was over, but because someone else thought I deserved something good. Someone besides Marcus and Scotty.

She turned to leave, and Detective Castillo took her place. He'd been there every step of the way, just like he'd promised, urging the DA to give Parker and me a break. It turned out that Parker knew more than I did, and he was perfectly willing to share the information once he knew I was safe. But none of it would have been possible without Raul Castillo. His had been the voice on the other end of the phone when I'd had no one else.

"I can never thank you enough," I said.

He shook his head. "It was all you. And I have a feeling this is just the beginning; you're going to do great things."

"You think so?" I asked.

He smiled. "I know so."

We promised to keep in touch, and then Scotty was there, pulling me into his arms in a giant bear hug. I held on tight, trying to memorize the feeling of being loved and protected, of being safe.

"I'm so proud of you, honey," he said.

"I couldn't have done it without you."

He pulled back to look at my face. "You could have and you would have, I have no doubt about that. But I'm glad we were here to help."

He stepped aside for Marcus, in his dress chinos and a freshly pressed shirt in yellow and orange that made him look like a tropical fruit salad. He grinned. "We did it, kid."

I smiled. "We did."

We stood there for a minute, grinning at each other like idiots.

"Oh, for Christ's sake," he said, grabbing me for a hug. I laughed into his shoulder. "Let's get out of here," he said. "This place gives me the creeps."

I grabbed my bag, and we headed for the hallway to wait for Parker. Marcus and Scotty were talking to the social worker when I heard a soft voice behind me.

"Grace."

I turned to see Leslie Fairchild, clutching her handbag.

"Mrs. Fairchild," I said. "Hello."

I don't know what I expected. She looked a lot like she had in December. Maybe she had a couple more wrinkles around her eyes, a little more gray in her hair, but her back was still straight, her gaze still strong. We had hurt the Fairchilds, but somehow I knew we hadn't beaten them. I was glad about that.

"I'm happy you have a chance to start again." She looked down at the purse in her hands before returning her eyes to mine. "I wanted to tell you I forgive you." She nodded, like she was pleased with the words she'd chosen. "I understand the predicament you were in, and I forgive you, Grace."

I shook my head. "Please don't make excuses for me," I said. "I hurt you and your family when you were nothing but kind to me. I'm so, so sorry for that. I know it doesn't change anything, but I want you to know it anyway."

"Thank you," she said.

"You didn't deserve what we did to you." I was still trying to reconcile all the things that happen to us in this life with my naive sense of justice. There didn't seem to be any rhyme or reason to it all. Bad stuff happened to good people, and just as often, it seemed like undeserving people got everything good. It made life that much harder to understand. Had I ended up in foster care because I'd been a bad kid? Even I knew that was unlikely. And the Fairchilds hadn't deserved what we'd done to them, either, however much Cormac tried to convince us otherwise. No one was guaranteed anything. That was the sad, scary, screwed-up, and, yes, beautiful truth of it. All we could do was keep our little corner of the world clean and hope for the best.

Leslie Fairchild smiled a little. "If only it were that simple." She took a deep breath. "I think . . . well, I think we're all just here to help each other figure things out."

"But we stole from you. Hurt you. Hurt your family."

"Yes, but I learned something, too." She didn't wait for me to ask to give the answer. "Logan and Warren and I are stronger than we knew. And I think that will make me a little less afraid from now on." I hardly had time to register my surprise—Leslie Fairchild had never seemed afraid to me—before she continued. "I wish you well, Grace. I hope that frees you somehow. It does me."

She gave me a quick hug and stepped aside. And then Logan was there. Right in front of me.

"Congratulations," he said. I shook my head. Despite the

fact that Parker was being released, today wasn't a congratulations type of day. "What will you do now?" he asked.

I shrugged. "Finish high school. Go on to college. Try to make up for what I've done." He nodded, his eyes burning into mine. He was beautiful. More than that, he was good and true. But all the magic that had been between us was gone, murdered by my own hand. "What about you?" I asked him.

"Summer, then college."

"Where are you going?" I asked. And then, because it had only just occurred to me: "If you want to tell me, I mean."

"USC," he said. "I need to try living out from under my dad's illness, but I also need to be close in case my mom needs me," he explained. "Which I guess doesn't make sense at all."

"It makes perfect sense," I said.

He shifted from one foot to the other. "Well, I better go."

"Take care, Logan."

His mother took his arm and they started down the hallway. They were almost to the elevator when he turned around. "Abbott, huh?"

I nodded.

He smiled just a little. "Good luck, Grace Abbott."

Forty-Two

I was packing up my things Sunday night when a knock sounded outside my door. It was late, too late to be Scotty or Marcus, which meant it had to be Parker.

We'd spent the last couple of days sitting outside in the hammock, watching the birds while we talked about the past few months. "Come in."

The door swung open and he stepped inside. I was still getting used to seeing him again. Sometimes I'd look at him and it seemed like the last seven months apart had been nothing but a bad dream. Other times, his presence made it even more real, and I'd have to stuff down my fear at the knowledge that we'd be separated again all too soon. I knew he'd visit me, but it would never be the same.

"Hey," I said, throwing my pajamas into the suitcase Scotty had insisted I keep. "Can't sleep?"

They'd given him back his bracelets when he'd been released, and the leather bands marched up his arm in familiar formation. The smudges under his eyes had faded a little, but he still looked haunted and a little off-balance. Scotty and Marcus had told him he could stay as long as he wanted. I hoped he would take them up on it. He was still too thin, and nothing could cure that problem like Scotty's cooking.

He sat down on the edge of my bed. "Grace . . ." He rubbed his hands on his thighs like he was trying to wipe his palms clean. "I'm leaving."

I scanned him for evidence that I'd misunderstood. It was only then that I saw the backpack in his hand. I sat down next to him.

"What do you mean?"

He shook his head. "I just . . . I need to get out of here. Scotty and Marcus are awesome, and I'm glad they've been here to take care of you. But I have to go."

"Go? Go where?" I was trying not to lose it as I thought of Parker getting farther and farther away from me all over again. "You're on probation. You can't just go."

He looked up at me. "Probation's just another prison. I can't spend the next five years checking in every week, picking up trash on the side of the road, explaining my record to everyone who interviews me for a minimum-wage job."

"Your record will be wiped clean if you meet the terms of the plea agreement."

He sighed. "I know. But it's not enough, Grace. I just . . . I can't live that way."

"Where will you go?" I asked. "What will you do?"

"I don't know." His shoulders lifted a little, and he almost smiled when he said it. "But I still have that money in my account from before. It's not a lot—it wouldn't even have paid for Kate Levy's retainer—but it'll get me out of the country, maybe to Mexico. After that, I'll make my way. Don't worry about me."

I shook my head. "You can't go. Not now, after everything that's happened." But I knew I was being selfish. I wouldn't even be in Playa Hermosa. What was he supposed to do? Hang around my new foster home? Live a life he hated while he waited around for me to finish college?

"Grace . . ." He reached out for my face, and I realized my cheeks were wet. "Don't cry. Please don't cry."

"You're not even going to ask me to come with you this time?"

He smiled a little. "No, because you deserve better, and you wouldn't come anyway. You already told me your plan: high school, college, a life of your own, an honest one. Remember? It's a good plan, Grace."

I realized with surprise that he was right. I'd outgrown my willingness to cling to the things that weren't good for me, even if they were the only things to hold on to, even if I loved them so much it hurt. Even if it was sad and scary to see them go.

I wrapped my arms around him and leaned my cheek on his chest. He smelled more like Parker now, but there was still something other, a scent that he'd picked up while we'd been apart. Maybe I smelled different, too.

"I'll miss you," I said.

"I'll miss you, too, Grace. But this isn't good-bye. I'll find you, wherever you are." He pulled back and looked at me. "We're family. It's always you and me. No matter what."

I nodded, choking on my tears, already feeling the loss of him. "No matter what."

"And if you need me," he said, "I'll be there. You can count on it."

We clung to each other like survivors of a shipwreck. I didn't try to hold back my tears. I was starting to think that life was a series of gains and losses. I guess Scotty would call it balance, but whatever it was, sometimes you needed to stop and mourn the things you lost along the way. It was a way of marking their presence, of acknowledging what they meant to you so you could finally take a step forward.

"Tell Scotty and Marcus thank you." Parker bent down, picked up his backpack, and headed for the door. When he got there, he turned around one last time. "I love you, Grace. Always have, always will."

A sob broke free of my throat. "I love you, too, Parker. Always have, always will."

And then he was gone.

My eyes were still red and raw the next morning when I put the last of my stuff into my suitcase and zipped it shut. Marcus and Scotty hadn't said much when I'd told them about Parker. Scotty's eyes had gotten a little wet when I started to cry, and he'd immediately pulled me into a hug. But Marcus hadn't looked all that surprised.

"Don't worry, kid," he'd said. "I know survivors, and Parker's a survivor if there ever was one."

Now I was bracing myself for another good-bye, repeating some of Scotty's mantras to keep myself from breaking down. How had I come to love him and Marcus so much? I couldn't imagine a day without Scotty's kindness, his steady presence. And what would I do without Marcus to make me laugh, to call me "kid" and remind me how funny life could be just when I needed it most?

I was getting ready to say good-bye to the birds when Scotty and Marcus came into my room.

"Hey, kid," Marcus said. He eyed my suitcase on the bed. "You might have jumped the gun on the packing."

"If I put it off any longer, you'll be shipping my stuff to Riverside," I said.

I didn't know much about my new foster family, but I'd been told they lived inland, about an hour and a half from the beach. I hated the thought of being away from the water, but it was the least of my worries, and Scotty and Marcus had promised to come get me for visits.

Scotty stepped toward me and took the backpack from my hands. He set it on the floor and smiled. "The thing is, honey, Marcus and I have been thinking. . . ."

Forty-Three

The sun was still hiding behind the marine layer when we stepped out of the courthouse three weeks later. Marcus put on his sunglasses as we made our way down the steps. He was wearing his chinos, but he looked good, and I'd gotten a little choked up when he'd come into the kitchen wearing a navy blue button-down. He'd squirmed as Scotty did one more button up near his neck, then stood back and smiled with approval.

"Don't get weird on me, Scott," Marcus had said, turning his back on us and hurrying to the coffeepot like he had something to hide.

I hadn't expected them to step in as my guardians at the last minute. Apparently, they'd been talking about it for a while, but they hadn't been able to reach a decision until the last minute. Not because they didn't want me to stay,

Scotty had assured me, but because Marcus was worried they wouldn't be able to give me the kind of parenting kids need. Scotty had argued that I was hardly a kid, and he and Marcus were as steady as an old married couple. In the end, according to Scotty, the decision had come down to one thing: neither of them wanted me to go.

I'd cried when they told me the news, then spent the next three weeks with an ever-present knot of anxiety in my stomach, worrying that it would somehow go wrong, that they would change their minds, that the court would deny their petition.

But everything had gone off without a hitch. I was old enough to have some say in my living situation, and I'd been given permission to stay with them while the court reviewed their petition. Now it was official: they were my guardians. That was what it said on the paperwork, anyway. In my eyes—and most importantly, my heart—they were my parents. And this time I knew it was for real.

"Well, kid," Marcus said, draping an arm around my shoulder as we headed for the car, "you're stuck with us now. And you know what that means."

"Back to the Hawaiian shirts?"

"Well, yes, there is that. Also," Marcus said, "there's the slave labor. I think we forgot to tell you about that."

"Slave labor?"

He nodded. "Kitchen detail, feeding the birds, you know . . . all that responsibility stuff that we're supposed to teach you."

"I'm okay with responsibility stuff," I said.

The attendant pulled the car around and we got in. We went out to breakfast, then headed home. The house on the peninsula wouldn't be ours much longer. Scotty and Marcus had decided it would be better for me to start fresh. They'd chosen Huntington Beach, and had already made an offer on a house there with a backyard big enough for all of Marcus's flowers and bird feeders. Best of all, the beach was a block away. We'd walked right down to the water the last time we'd seen the house, and I'd watched the surfers catching waves and the girls playing volleyball and wondered which of them I would come to know when I started school next month. Then again, maybe I wouldn't know any of them. Maybe I'd become friends with a quiet girl who sat alone and liked to read instead.

"Take the afternoon off, kid," Marcus said as we walked into the house on Colina Verde. "We'll get you started in the salt mines tomorrow."

"Ha-ha," I said, heading up the stairs to my room.

I changed into shorts and a tank top and grabbed my book. Then I went to the kitchen and poured a glass of iced tea before heading to the backyard.

It was finally sunny, and I could hear the waves crashing against the cliffs as I walked barefoot to the hammock. For a while I just lay there, swinging in the sea breeze, inhaling the scent of jasmine and salt and fresh-cut grass. One of the hummingbirds was fluttering around the red bird feeder, moving so fast I almost thought it was a figment of my imagination. It made me think of the peacocks. Like me, they were on their way somewhere else. A majority of the residents of Playa Hermosa had voted to have them moved, and they were already en route to the animal sanctuary that would be their new home. When I'd first heard the news, I'd felt bad for them. But then I started to wonder if maybe they needed a fresh start, too. If maybe home wasn't a place you knew, but a place where you were always welcome.

A flash of yellow caught my eye in the trees overhead. I laid my book facedown on my chest and peered through the branches, looking for the parrots. A few seconds later they appeared. The one with the yellow eyes was still the most aggressive, and the other birds hung back, letting him take his turn at the feeder first. When he was done, he perched on the branch of a nearby tree. It was only then that his companions—the one with the red head and the other one with blue-tipped wings—appeared. They were still pecking at the seed when a fourth bird landed next to them. His blue body stood in contrast to the green bodies of the others, and they paused to look at him before turning back to their food as the newcomer picked at the feeder alongside them. I guess he'd found a home, too.

I took a deep breath, releasing it into the salty Playa Hermosa air. It felt like I'd been holding that breath forever. Like I was finally letting go of all my pain and fear and loneliness, of everything that had kept me from fighting for the things I wanted and deserved. But in a strange kind of way, I thought everything had turned out the way it was supposed to. Everything finally felt right. I guess Scotty knew what he was talking about after all, although he had been wrong about one thing: sometimes, if you were really, really lucky, more than one good thing came out of a bad situation. I only had to look at Marcus and Scotty to know that at least two good things had come out of mine.

I thought about Parker, probably on a beach in Mexico, sipping a beer and looking at the same ocean that crashed against the cliffs below me. I missed him, but I knew with a strange kind of certainty that I would see him again. He was my family, simple as that, and family was always a part of you. We could both rest easy now. He was free, and I had kept my promise to come back for him.

Now it was time to keep the ones I'd made to myself.

Acknowledgments

Thanks always start with Steven Malk and all of the amazing people at Writers House, for seeing me safely through troubled waters and never doubting that I would make it—even when I wasn't so sure.

Thanks also go to my editor, Jennifer Klonsky. Just when I was starting to think publishing was impossibly disheartening, ridiculously unreliable, and most of all, SLOW, I was given an editor who is kind, encouraging, and on her game every minute of every day. At a time when it sometimes feels like publishers won't invest in an author's long-term career, you have made me believe again. After working with you for the past year and a half, I'm finally starting to think that's not naïvety talking, but bona fide faith.

Thank you to HarperCollins Publishers and everyone at HarperTeen who have made me feel welcome and valued.

This is especially true for publicist Stephanie Hoover and associate editor Catherine Wallace, who see to tons of important stuff behind the scenes that nobody sees. Thanks also to Alison Klapthor, Alison Donalty, and Sarah Kaufman for another kickass cover (and for actually letting me be part of the process), and to copy editors Karen Sherman and Bethany Reis, who put me through my paces to make sure this book was as solid and accurate as possible. Any errors are totally mine.

Thanks to dear friends M. J. Rose, Tonya Hurley, Ann Rought, Jenny Milchman, Christine Fonseca, Erin Leigh Brescia, Eileen Cole, Jennifer Draeger, and so many more who share this beautiful and sometimes maddening journey to deliver our words to readers, and to those readers who buy my books, and therefore keep me writing. You are the biggest contributors of all.

Lastly, thanks go to the people who are the backbone of my life: my mother, Claudia Baker, for her unwavering faith in me; my father, Mike St. James, who reminds me that I've already done something pretty cool (we need to be reminded sometimes!); and Kenneth, Rebekah, Andrew, and Caroline. If there is universal truth, beauty, and love in my life, it is you.